Time Stops for No Mouse

A Hermux Tantamoq Adventure™

MICHAEL HOEYE

PUFFIN BOOKS

PUFFIN BOOKS

Published by the Penguin Group
Penguin Books Ltd, 80 Strand, London WC2R 0RL, England
Penguin Putnam Inc., 375 Hudson Street, New York, New York 10014, USA
Penguin Books Australia Ltd, 250 Camberwell Road, Camberwell, Victoria 3124, Australia
Penguin Books Canada Ltd, 10 Alcorn Avenue, Toronto, Ontario, Canada M4V 3B2
Penguin Books India (P) Ltd, 11 Community Centre, Panchsheel Park,
New Delhi – 110 017, India
Penguin Books (NZ) Ltd, Cnr Rosedale and Airborne Roads, Albany, Auckland, New Zealand
Penguin Books (South Africa) (Pty) Ltd, 24 Sturdee Avenue, Rosebank 2196, South Africa

Penguin Books Ltd, Registered Offices: 80 Strand, London WC2R 0RL, England

www. penguin.com

Writer's first proof edition (1000) copyright © Michael Hoeye 1999, 2000
First published in Great Britain 2002
1

Text copyright © Michael Hoeye, 1999
Book design and cover art created by Dale Champlin, copyright © Terfle House Limited, 2000
A Hermux Tantamoq Adventure is a trademark of Terfle House Limited
Rated: Not Too Scary is a servicemark of Terfle House Limited
All rights reserved

The moral right of the author has been asserted

Set in Cochin
Made and printed in England by Clays Ltd, St Ives plc

British Library Cataloguing in Publication Data
A CIP catalogue record for this book is available from the British Library

ISBN 0 670 91306 5

PUFFIN BOOKS

Time Stops for No Mouse

Michael Hoeye is inventive and an excellent writer. *Time Stops for No Mouse* is a complex tale involving secret formulas, the evil mole Doctor Mennus and his rat henchman, a missing adventuress and hotel redecoration. He has created in the watchmaker mouse Hermux Tantamoq an unlikely but truly captivating hero. As for his friend Linka Perflinger (whose business card reads, 'adventuress, daredevil and aviatrix'), we want to see more of her, too.

– ANN WALDRON, *PHILADELPHIA INQUIRER*

This is possibly the most delightful book I have ever fondled and perused. Once people pick it up and begin to read, they cannot resist it.

– BOBBIE TICHENOR, *BOOK SENSE 76*

ANNIE BLOOM'S BOOKS, PORTLAND, OREGON

For readers of all ages! If you enjoy Brian Jacques or E.B. White, you've got to read *Time Stops for No Mouse*. 'Not too scary' but plenty suspenseful – it will keep you guessing and smiling all the way through. *Time Stops for No Mouse* is funny and touching, and it carries important lessons about beauty, growing old and acceptance.

– JODY FOSTER

DAVINCI MIDDLE SCHOOL, PORTLAND, OREGON

This book is dedicated to my beloved wife,
Martha Ann Banyas.
True friend and true heart.

Chapter 1
An Unexpected Visit

'Oh my! Oh my!' murmured Hermux Tantamoq as he carefully examined the wristwatch. He had never seen such a beautiful watch so badly treated. The crystal was shattered. The hands were twisted like melted wax. The face was chipped and scratched so badly that the numbers were barely legible.

The young mouse drummed the countertop with her sharp nails.

'Please get this repaired immediately,' she said in a rush. 'It must keep perfect time. Perfect. Nothing less!'

Hermux removed his eyepiece and stared at his impatient new customer.

Her face was set in a sharp frown, but it was such a jolly, bright face that the frown looked out of place. She wore no make-up. Just her natural fur. A dark glossy brown. She had on a red cap with a bright green feather in its brim, a jaunty, checked scarf, and a somewhat worn-looking leather flight jacket.

From the depths of her shoulder-bag she withdrew a small

case. From that she removed a violet-tinted business card which she presented to Hermux with a flourish.

'Please send the bill to this address.'

Ms Linka Perflinger
Adventuress, Daredevil and Aviatrix
Bold Feats of Nerve and Verve
On Land and In the Air
Reasonable Rates
3 Pickdorndle Lane
Pinchester

Hermux placed the wristwatch carefully on the velvet tray and studied the card.

'This watch is very nearly ruined, Ms Perflinger. It will take a miracle to fix it completely,' he told her in his most serious voice. 'Of course,' he added with a note of pride, 'I am accustomed to performing such miracles. When do you need it done?'

'Why, this afternoon, of course! Time is money. I can't afford to be without time for an entire day!'

'My dear Ms Perflinger, I'm afraid it is quite impossible that I fix it today. To begin with, there is Cladenda Noddem's grandfather clock. I shall have to make an entirely new trindle-spring for it from scratch. Then there is Bratchlin Weffup's pocket watch which I promised him a week ago. He's bent the winding stem as crooked as a turnip. And I shall have to pound it out straight. And grind it. And polish it smooth again. And then there's your watch, Ms Perflinger! What a shock to see

2

such a beautiful watch as this in such a dreadful state of disrepair. What on earth has happened?'

'Occupational hazard. That's all!' she said brusquely. 'I'm not at liberty to say more. But I will say this. The profession of adventuress, which I follow, appears to operate on whim and derring-do, but it is based almost entirely on precision timing. On careful planning. And meticulous execution. This watch that you see in its broken and battered state is as much a part of me as my own pulse. I can assure you that I took every possible precaution to avoid this disagreeable damage. And I can also assure you that I need it keeping perfect time in order to return to my work. And that said, when can you have it fixed?'

Hermux replaced his eyepiece and studied the watch. 'Naturally I shall have to replace the crystal.'

'Naturally,' responded Ms Perflinger.

'Of course, I shall have to replace the twisted hands,' continued Hermux.

'Of course,' answered Ms Perflinger.

'I will undoubtedly have to resurface the face and re-paint the numbers,' added Hermux. 'And I will have to do that with the smallest paintbrush imaginable.'

'Undoubtedly,' said Ms Perflinger.

'And most definitely the mechanism will have to be cleaned, and oiled and adjusted at the very least,' he concluded.

'Most definitely,' agreed Ms Perflinger.

'Perhaps late tomorrow morning, if this is, indeed, an emergency.'

'An emergency of the most compelling sort,' murmured Ms Perflinger gratefully.

Hermux filled out the repair tag in his careful, small handwriting. He tied it securely to the watch. Then he tore off the receipt and handed it to Ms Perflinger.

'Tomorrow, then,' he said with his small smile. 'Right before lunch.'

'Tomorrow,' she repeated. And then turned to leave. At the door, she turned back to him with a worried look. 'It must keep perfect time,' she said gravely. 'Even a second can mean the difference between life and death.'

After she left, Hermux set right to work.

He took the watch over to his workbench and adjusted the light. Using fine pointed tweezers, he removed each sliver of broken crystal. Then he took a tiny pair of pliers and detached the delicate hands, placing them in a small glass dish. He pried off the back of the watch and examined the inside. He stopped occasionally as he worked and made notes in his notebook.

Chapter 2
A FUR-RAISING ENCOUNTER

It was quite late when Hermux arrived home that night. He got the mail from his mailbox and thumbed through it as he waited for the old elevator to lumber its way down to the lobby. The ride up was even slower, but he didn't care. He was looking forward to a nice bowl of soup and a quiet, pleasant evening of reading.

On the fourth floor the elevator let out a rusty creak, an oily thunk, a shivery shudder, and then yanked to a stop. Hermux pushed carefully on the elevator door, opening it just a crack. Then he poked his nose out stealthily and peered down the hall. The door to Tucka Mertslin's apartment was closed.

He stepped out of the elevator and crept towards the door to his apartment as quietly as a mouse.

He carefully took out his ring of keys. He sorted past the silver key to his bicycle, the round key to his store, the little gold key to his safe, the silvery square-topped key to his locker at the gymnasium, the oval-shaped key to his filing cabinet, and finally reached the double-sided brass key that opened the door to his apartment.

He slipped the key carefully into the lock and turned it cautiously.

'Why Hermux Tantamoq! Sneaking past my door like a burglar!' scolded someone directly behind him.

Hermux whirled around in terror. There was Tucka Mertslin standing not one step away. A great fog of perfume enveloped her and was now working its way into every crevice in the hallway. A cloud of it settled on Hermux, tickling his nose like a longhaired squirrel tail. It was a horrid smell, like flowers that had been trampled to death in a sweet shop.

Tucka towered over Hermux in her pink and green lizard-skin platform shoes. A huge cone-shaped hat added even more to her height. From the top of her hat sprang a fountain of metallic ribbons that fell past her waist. The shiny ribbons swirled about her body like a swarm of hungry eels and made it difficult to see her face clearly. What he could see of it was unsettling.

Tucka's cheeks were dusted with a fine orange powder that gave her fur the appearance of being on fire. The whiskers above her smallish eyes had been extended so dramatically that they bobbed about like antennae, nearly tangling in the ribbons. Her lips were drawn coal black, shiny and glistening. She smiled at him dangerously.

'I suppose you didn't get my invitation?' she said. 'I distinctly said the meeting would begin at six o'clock. It was quite productive actually. A pity you missed it. But then I suppose you had more important things to do. In any case decisions have been made. And you'll be seeing some real changes around here starting quite soon.'

'Changes?' asked Hermux. 'In what?'

'In the hallway, you dunce,' she continued irritably. 'I'm

heading up the Subcommittee for Hall Decoration. Or have you forgotten that too?'

At that Hermux let out a tremendous sneeze that shook the iridescent ruffles on Tucka's low-cut blouse. It was a wet, splashy sort of sneeze. The kind you hope you can aim into a handkerchief. But it happened so fast, it surprised even Hermux.

'You horrible little ... rodent!' Tucka hissed, dabbing her face with a bit of spider lace. 'You nasty little vermin! In any case I've given you fair warning. Decisions have been made. Made and seconded. And passed unanimously. Now stay–out–of–my–way! And you can start by getting this hideous umbrella stand out of my hall.'

With that she aimed a sharp kick at the rocket-ship umbrella stand that Hermux had brought back from his trip to the World's Fair when he was a boy.

As her foot flashed by in front of him, Hermux said, 'I wish you wouldn't do that.'

Tucka's shriek shattered the air.

'It's made of lead,' he continued.

'You've broken my foot!' she bellowed, lurching back and shaking her fist under Hermux's nose. She turned in a fury and limped away. 'You'll hear about this from my lawyers!' she shouted. 'You'll pay every cent!'

'Every cent of what, I wonder,' sighed Hermux. He set his umbrella stand back upright, opened the door to his apartment, and stepped gratefully inside. He locked the lock. He threw the deadbolt. He fastened the chain. And for extra measure he peered through the peephole and watched until Tucka vanished completely from sight. 'That woman will drive me nuts!'

T

Chapter 3
THE COMFORTS OF HOME

Hermux threw the mail on his desk in his study and promptly forgot all about Tucka Mertslin.

He ran to the front window and peered into the cage where his pet ladybird dozed quietly on her perch. 'Wake up, Terfle!' he said merrily. 'I'm home.' He reached through the bars of the cage and stroked the edge of her glossy red wing. Terfle opened and closed her wings and stretched up in a lazy yawn.

'How was your day?' Hermux asked. 'Mine was most peculiar, I can tell you that! Right up until this very moment. And it's wonderful to be home!' He opened the tin of dried aphids and shook a handful into Terfle's bowl. She leapt down on to the floor of her cage and began greedily to eat.

Hermux watched happily. 'Home, where no one snoops! And no one shouts!' he shouted. 'Except me, of course!' He spun around and leapt high into the air with a little twist and a wiggle. And landed with a crash that nearly knocked Terfle's cage off its stand.

'And now for supper!' he announced and got back to his feet.

In the kitchen Hermux opened the refrigerator and removed a pot of soup and set it to heat. Then he changed out of his shop clothes. He removed his jacket and carefully brushed it before putting it on its wooden hanger. He untied his bow tie. He unbuttoned his shirt and took it off. He examined its collar carefully for dirt and sniffed cautiously under the arms. 'I think it still has one more good day left in it,' he said and hung it up carefully. He untied his shoes, and set them beside his bed to air. From his chest of drawers he took out a pair of thick woollen socks and slipped them over his dress socks. He took down a flannel shirt printed all over with pictures of cheeses from around the world. Then he put on his house shoes and his thick, fuzzy dressing gown, and walked back to the kitchen.

The soup was bubbling furiously on the stove. He turned it off and took down from the cabinet a large bowl the colour of a midnight sky. Around its rim marched a line of white ducks drawn with egg-yolk yellow feet and bills and jet black eyes.

'Watch out, ducks!' cried Hermux, ladling the steaming soup into the bowl. He carried the soup to the table, got down a box of crackers, poured himself a glass of milk and sat down to eat.

'My!' he said to himself. 'This was a very unusual day. That was a narrow escape with Tucka Mertslin. And that Miss Perflinger is quite a dynamic mouse. Quite unlike anyone I've met before!' He remembered her bright, outgoing face, her slightly crooked nose, and the musical but very determined sound of her voice. Then he added, 'But she is certainly quite like someone I'd like to meet again.'

9

After he'd washed his dishes and set them to dry, Hermux prepared himself a pot of tea. And while it steeped, he peeled a small apple, sliced it into thin wedges, and cut himself a sizeable piece of sharp, crumbly cheese, nibbling only the tiniest amount. He arranged everything on the table beside his reading chair in the study. He lit a small fire in the fireplace. Then he settled himself comfortably in his chair, put on his glasses and began to read his mail.

First was a picture postcard showing the milking room at a cheese factory in Grebbenland. It was from his cousin Tannik, who was there on his honeymoon. Hermux held the card up so Terfle could get a good look at it. 'It's from Tannik and Vinnapy,' he explained. 'They're having a wonderful time. The cheese is superb. They hope I'm feeding you well. They are bringing you some special treats.'

Next was a letter from his friend Nip Setchley, who wanted Hermux to invest in Nip's newest idea, a caravan-park resort that moved from place to place like a motel on wheels. 'Never gets boring,' Nip promised. Hermux had never known him to lack enthusiasm. And it did sound rather exciting. A new place every day. But the same people. Adventurous but cosy at the same time.

'I'll have to give that some thought,' said Hermux and turned his attention to a small blue envelope of thin tissue. A vaguely familiar scent wafted up to Hermux's sensitive nose as he tore it open. Flowers. Hundreds of bruised and tortured flowers seemed to explode in the air. And something sugary and rotten. The card inside was embossed with a bold TM.

'Tucka Mertslin!' he muttered.

'The twenty-third of March. That was today!' he admitted,

> *Miss Tucka Mertslin*
> *Chairwoman*
> *Subcommittee for Hall Decoration*
> *requests the pleasure of your company*
> *on Monday, the twenty-third of March*
> *at six o'clock*
> *at her residence*
> *to view drawings and plans for*
> *new hallway décor.*

embarrassed. 'No wonder she was steamed. But when did she mail it?' He studied the postmark on the envelope. It was marked 22 March.

'Yesterday. Not likely I'd get it in time to attend her meeting and be disruptive,' he thought. 'But then I doubt that Miss Mertslin actually wanted me there at all. And now that she thinks she's got me out of the picture, she can carry out her redecoration plans without any interference from me.

'Looks like it might be war, Terfle,' he announced grimly. 'The war of the wallpaper.' And with that he ate a wedge of apple, two pieces of cheese, poured himself a cup of tea, and opened the new edition of the *Weekly Squeak*.

As usual the news was mixed. Good things had happened to bad people. Bad things had happened to good people.

Several surprising new things had been discovered. Quite a few old things had been damaged. Trouble was brewing on one horizon. And peace had been reached on another. The short-term forecast was growth. The long-term forecast was shrinkage. The days were getting colder. But temperatures were rising in general. And then he saw her picture.

She was standing beside an aeroplane on a landing strip in some sort of jungle.

Chapter 4
A FAMILIAR FACE

It was Ms Perflinger. Her arm was raised to shield her eyes from the sun. Her face was hidden in shadow. But there was no doubt about it. Ms Perflinger. The same jaunty checked scarf. The same shoulder-bag. The same tilt of the head. It was her.

Hermux read the article in a rush.

BOLD MOVE BY BRAVE FLYER SAVES DAY FOR TROUBLED EXPEDITION

—Aviatrix Linka Perflinger landed safely today after a nerve-racking solo flight across the Gulf of Tretch on a daring mission bringing much-needed supplies to Dr Turfip Dandiffer's troubled ethnobotanical exploration of the Teulabonari Rainforest.

'It was touch and go there for a while,' the exhausted flyer reported. 'I nearly bagged it in a waterspout. My controls jammed. My radio went out. I got roughed up pretty badly. But knowing how critical it was, I hung in there. Now the supplies are safely delivered, and Dr Dandiffer can return to his important work.'

Back in the city, a spokesperson for the Perriflot Institute, sponsor of the Dandiffer expedition, held a press conference to announce Perflinger's success. 'On behalf of Ortolina Perriflot, the richest woman in the world, and the Perriflot Institute, we would like to express our appreciation to Ms Perflinger. We are confident that Dr Dandiffer can now complete his crucial mission. And that he will soon return to us with discoveries that will change the course of modern medicine.' The spokesperson would not elaborate further on the nature of Dandiffer's work.

Asked about her plans for the immediate future, Linka Perflinger declined to comment. 'All I can promise is I'll be taking a long hot bath as soon as I get home. Then a wash, a wax and a tune-up for my plane. And I'll need to get my watch fixed.'

'Ah, yes!' mused Hermux dreamily. 'The watch! Battered by a storm.'

Hermux took down his world atlas and thumbed through the pages. There it was—the Gulf of Tretch. It was bigger than he remembered. And to the south of that the Teulabonari Rainforest. With the exception of the Bonari Mountains and two large rivers that snaked their ways through the rainforest and emptied into the Gulf, the map was blank.

Where in all that jungle had Ms Perflinger landed? he wondered.

That night as he brushed his teeth he studied himself in the mirror over the sink. He was definitely looking more mature. Not quite old, he decided. But he did detect just the slightest hint of droop at the tips of his whiskers. He pulled them out straight and released them. There was definitely a hint of droop. 'Nothing, mind you, that a bit of Flip wax can't handle,' he told himself, turning out the light. He retired to his bedroom, took his sleeping-cap off its hook on the inside of his closet door, pulled it snugly over his ears, and crawled into bed.

'Gracious,' he murmured. 'I feel like I could sleep for a week.' But no sooner had he switched off the light than he began to think.

He thought about aeroplanes. And storm clouds. And wild winds. And flying through the night. In pitch darkness. With sea foam and tossing waves below.

He thought about platform shoes. And lizards. And decorators with great bolts of chintz. And swag and wallpaper paste and blueprints.

He thought about jaunty scarves and hats with feathers. And bright faces. And steaming green jungles. And committee meetings.

And the smell of jungle flowers.

He thought about life and death. And romance. And chandeliers. And orange-tinted facial fur.

He thought about broken watches. With twisted hands that went around and around and around. And the drone of a tiny red aeroplane in a bright blue sky that got closer and closer and closer.

And suddenly it was morning. And his alarm clock buzzed mightily beside him.

Chapter 5
ALL IN A DAY'S WORK

Hermux rushed downtown. He unlocked the shop. He flipped the sign on the door from *Closed* to *Open*. He turned on the lights. He raised the window blinds. He removed the brown flannel covers from the display cases. He switched on the lamp over his workbench, took out the tray that held Ms Perflinger's watch, and, setting his magnifying eyepiece carefully into his right eye, he set to work.

The damage was worse than he had thought. The mainspring was sprung. The balance was unbalanced. The escape wheel had escaped. Gears had been stripped. Parts would have to be replaced. Some parts he would have to make. It would be a hard morning's work.

It was already ten o'clock the first time that Hermux looked up. He sat up straight and rubbed his neck. He looked at the notes in his notebook. A column of black ticks was growing alongside the list of problems he had written out. He added another firm tick. And then stood up.

'It's time for coffee!' he said. He put on his hat and his

coat. And used a clothespeg to fasten a small hand-lettered card over the *Open* sign.

Will return shortly.

Morning coffee was Hermux's favourite time of the day. It was when he did his best thinking. His best chatting. His best daydreaming. His best doodling. And his best people-watching.

And this morning, Hermux had a lot to think about. A lot to chat about. And a lot to daydream about.

Lanayda Prink made the best coffee downtown. And that was where Hermux headed.

'One coffee. Regular. No sugar,' Lanayda yelled as soon as Hermux stepped inside her coffee shop.

Hermux squeezed on to a seat at the counter. His feet barely reached the foot-rail. 'What kind of doughnuts do you have this morning?' he asked brightly.

'We've got plain and glazed. Cake and raised. Chocolate and coconut. Maple and walnut,' Lanayda told him.

'In that case, I'll have a plain, cake, chocolate doughnut. For here.'

'Plain, cake, chocolate. For here!' Lanayda yelled and moments later a white china saucer holding a plain, cake, chocolate doughnut slid on to the counter through a slot in the wall. It was followed by a steaming mug of coffee. Regular, no sugar. Lanayda slid them both down to Hermux.

'You're looking chipper this morning, Hermux,' she smiled. 'Business must be booming.'

'Not booming exactly,' he answered. 'But blooming. Certainly blooming.'

He sipped his coffee happily. Dark and bitter. And then he took a small bite of doughnut and let the sweet chocolate drive the bitterness away.

'You know, Lanayda,' he told her, 'meeting the public ... that's the thing! Having unusual people walk in from the street with no warning. And pop! You're swept into a world you've never even imagined. Miles from home. Hundreds of feet in the air. On a dangerous mission. Fighting for your life.'

But just then the door opened. It was Earlin Bray, the lawyer. Lanayda waved at Earlin and yelled, 'Coffee. Light and sweet! Doughnut. Glazed and raised. To go!' She met Earlin at the cash register as a paper cup and doughnut in a waxed paper bag slid out of the slot.

Hermux closed his eyes and pictured Ms Perflinger high above the Gulf of Tretch, buffeted by winds, fog covering her windshield, her engine coughing and sputtering, her beautiful watch stopped at twelve o'clock sharp.

He opened his eyes.

'Goodness!' he said. 'I'd better get back to work!'

Chapter 6
THE WAITING GAME

It was five minutes before twelve o'clock noon. Hermux glanced up quickly at the clock. He was nearly finished with Linka Perflinger's beautiful wristwatch. He had cleaned, oiled, and rebuilt its movement. He had carefully repainted the Roman numerals on its face with the smallest paintbrush imaginable. He had chosen new hands to replace the ones that had been mangled and twisted. And now he was setting them in place and attaching them to the driveshaft.

Moments later he placed the crystal cover in its gold setting and snapped it on to the watch. Done!

And with two minutes to spare!

He let out a great sigh of relief and closed his tired eyes a moment to imagine the frowning face of Linka Perflinger transformed by a smile of gratitude.

He opened his eyes. Still one minute to go. Ms Perflinger was certainly the punctual type. He expected the door to be flung open promptly at noon. Give or take a second.

Only thirty seconds remaining. He wondered if she would be wearing her red hat with the green feather. If her red and white checked scarf would be thrown so jauntily over her shoulders. If she would share some of the details of her marvellous flying adventure.

It was twelve o'clock exactly.

And then it was one minute past twelve precisely.

And then it was two minutes past. On the dot.

And then three.

Hermux stood at the window and peered up and down the street. Across the street Teasila Tentriff, the dance teacher, was unlocking the entrance to the Tentriff Academy of Dance and Theatrics. Quendle Tiptorf was just coming out of the barber's on the corner. And Tratin Dilmo was running for the bus. But there was no sign of Ms Perflinger.

Hermux checked the door to the shop to make sure the sign said *Open*. From the cabinet by his desk he removed a dark green box embossed with the words

Hermux Tantamoq Watchmaker

in flowing gold script. He took off the lid and set Ms Perflinger's watch very carefully on to the bed of snow-white cotton inside. He closed the box and set it on the counter by the cash register where he stood and waited.

At one o'clock he opened his lunch bag. He poured a glass of apple juice from his Thermos and ate a stick of celery. But the stinky cheese sandwich and the butterscotch pudding and the peanut brittle and the banana he left. He wasn't hungry.

At two o'clock the door opened, and Hermux jumped to attention.

'Ms Perflinger!' he sputtered.

But it was Cladenda Noddem and her naughty little boy Nock.

'Mrs Noddem, I'm sorry. I was expecting someone.'

'I assume you are also expecting me, Mr Tantamoq,' teased Mrs Noddem. 'My claim ticket says Tuesday afternoon. And today is Tuesday. And it's after noon. So here I am to see what marvels you've done to grandfather's clock. And I've brought Nock here so you can explain to him yourself why it is that he cannot ride the pendulum. Nor play the chimes with his drumsticks. Nor swing on the chains. Nor use the weights for bowling pins. He will not believe me or his father.'

And so Hermux explained to Nock why he should not do any of the above. And showed him the trindle-spring that Nock had broken. And demonstrated how he had made a new one by bending a narrow band of steel around and around a steel pin to form a spiral. But Nock wasn't interested in the least. Until, that is, Hermux showed him how to use a tiny key to open the door at the base of the clock and use a flashlight to light up the whirring gears and spinning wheels inside. Nock was clearly fascinated by the workings of the clock.

As they were leaving Hermux thought that maybe the lad wasn't all bad, as he had heard. But while they stood in the doorway and Hermux told Mrs Noddem that Nock might have the makings of an engineer or even a watchmaker, Nock was already imagining using the gears of his grandfather's clock to roll a penny into a zigzag shape. And wondering how much his friends would pay for a special zigzag penny when just yesterday he had paid five cents for one that had only been flattened by a train.

By five o'clock it was clear that Ms Perflinger was not

coming. Hermux stepped outside the shop and looked up and down the street. And looked again. Just to be sure.

Then he went inside. He carefully taped Ms Perflinger's work ticket to the bottom of the watch-box. He took one last look at the watch. The polished gold case, the crystal-clear crystal, the pearl-white face, the crisp black numerals, the sharp silver hands that said 'five o'clock' exactly.

'It is perfect,' he sighed. 'Just as she asked.'

He closed the box and placed it on the shelf marked 'Will Call' right next to Bratchlin Weffup's pocket watch.

Then he turned out the lights and locked up his shop and went home.

Chapter 7
FINDING THE RIGHT WORDS

A week went by, and there was no word from Linka Perflinger. No call. No message. When he thought of her, and he thought of her often, Hermux didn't know whether to be worried or angry. At heart he felt that something serious must have happened to keep her from returning for her watch as she had promised. But he hated to think of anything serious happening to Linka Perflinger.

On the other hand, if nothing serious had happened to her, then she was rude and irresponsible for making him work so hard to meet her deadline and then not even bothering to pick up her watch. What if she had bought a new watch instead? It made Hermux mad just to think about it. And he didn't want to be mad at Linka Perflinger.

Hermux was in what he called a dilemma. He didn't want to think about her because it upset him. But he didn't want to not think about her either. She had seemed like such a decent sort of mouse. No, she seemed more than decent. She was full of life and determination. She was full of adventure.

He decided to write her a letter.

He opened his desk drawer and took out a sheet of writing paper.

My dear Ms Perflinger, he began.

I worked very hard to fix your watch. And I had better things to do I can tell you. I barely had time to fix Cladenda Noddem's clock. I was late for my dinner. And I missed an important committee meeting called to determine the decoration scheme of my apartment building which I will have to live with for years to come. You have not picked up your watch. And you haven't paid me either.

Sincerely,

Before he signed it, he stopped and read what he had written.

'That doesn't sound very nice,' he told himself. 'Perhaps a softer tone.' He tore up the letter and took out another sheet of paper.

Dear Linka, he wrote.

I am worried that something awful has happened to you. If you are in trouble, please remember that you have a friend in

Hermux Tantamoq

P.S. Your watch is ready.

He studied the letter. 'Maybe that's just a wee bit too desperate,' he thought. He tore it up and took out another sheet of paper.

Dear Ms Perflinger, he wrote.

Perhaps you have forgotten your watch which you left with me to be repaired. I believe you will be pleased to know that it has been fully restored to working order and that it is once again keeping perfect time.

You may call for it at your earliest convenience.

Yours truly,
Hermux Tantamoq

'There,' he said, satisfied. 'Not too sour. And not too sweet.'

He folded the letter and slipped it into an envelope. He copied her address from her card. He closed up the shop and walked immediately to the post office and mailed it.

'The important thing is to do something,' he said to himself, coming back. 'It's the sitting and waiting that wears one down.'

As he walked along the busy street he was greeted by a curious apparition. A tall mouse wearing an odd hat shaped like a pair of bat wings hobbled towards him, clumsily supporting herself with two canes. Her feet and ankles were encased in bandages and she seemed to be walking on the very tips of her toes.

'She must have had a nasty fall,' thought Hermux. And then he recognized her. It was Tucka. Without thinking, he rushed towards her.

'Ms Mertslin! My goodness! I am so awfully sorry! I had no idea!' he stammered.

Tucka balanced herself with her canes and peered down at

26

him. 'What on earth are you babbling about?' she demanded.

'Your feet,' he said desperately. 'The umbrella stand. I'm afraid you've broken your ankles.'

'Mr Tantamoq, you're an even bigger idiot than I supposed. I have not broken my ankles. I am advocating a more ethereal approach to footwear. I am evoking an image of weightlessness and fragility.'

'But you look very uncomfortable doing it.'

'You simply don't get it, do you?' said Tucka, adjusting her canes a moment. 'Beauty is discipline. The creation of the rare and the improbable. I am beginning to believe that you are simply too narrow, too limited a soul to possess even the most rudimentary sense of beauty.'

And she dismissed him and continued on her way, tottering down the street, attracting the admiring stares of passers-by as she went.

Hermux was stung by her comment. 'Perhaps she's right. Perhaps I am narrow and limited,' he mused. 'I've always assumed I had a sense of beauty, but I've never given it much thought. I think that Terfle is beautiful with her bright wings and their brilliant black spots. I've always thought that the tower clock at Gurfenville is beautiful. Especially the way the bluebird flies away from its nest on the hour and returns on the half hour. And I certainly think that Ms Perflinger is beautiful.' And his heart skipped a beat at the thought of Ms Perflinger.

'But there's no point in thinking about that,' he told himself.

Chapter 8
RUMOURS OF ROMANCE

On the day he mailed his letter to Ms Perflinger, Hermux circled the date on his calendar in red ink. After that he waited each day for the mail to arrive.

Lista Blenwipple was Hermux's post-lady. She had delivered the mail downtown for as long as anyone could remember. She knew where every building was and every office in it. She knew who worked where and who got hired and who got fired. And she usually knew why.

Lista noticed right away that Hermux was anxious about a particular piece of mail. He met her every morning, stepping out of the shop door to greet her on the pavement.

'Good morning, Lista,' he beamed. 'What do you have for me today?'

'Why, Hermux, have you joined another book club? Or is it more jewels for your watches that you're expecting?'

'Actually, Lista, it's more of a personal nature,' he confided.

That was all Lista needed to hear. By that afternoon everyone downtown had heard that Hermux was waiting for a written answer to a proposal of marriage. No one, not even Lista, could venture a guess as to who the lucky mouse might be. But plans were definitely afoot. It would no doubt be a big wedding. With tons of food. And an enormous cake. And beautiful invitations. And a dance band. And speeches. And party favours. And flowers.

Hermux was no cheapskate.

It would probably be a June wedding. There was just enough time to get it organized properly. 'Organized like clockwork,' Lista would add. 'You can bet on that.'

It was exciting news. Calendars were checked. Conflicts were avoided. June must be kept free until the exact date was set. Some people left work early that day so they could shop for new party clothes before all the best ones in the brightest new colours were taken.

And so it was that every morning Lista Blenwipple gave Hermux an especially sympathetic smile when she handed him his mail. Because there was no special letter for him. And Lista could spot a special letter a mile away. There were just bills, and notices, and catalogues, and the *Watchmaker's Journal*.

'Not today, dear,' she would say to Hermux reassuringly. 'But very soon I'm sure.'

Chapter 9
IN THE DUMPS

'Stop!' shouted Hermux, breaking into a frantic run. 'Stop at once! Stop!' His voice rose in a wail as he raced from the corner to the doorway of his apartment building.

Hermux crashed into the large beaver who was tossing broken furniture and wood into a skip parked on the street.

'What do you think you're doing?' Hermux demanded. He scrambled up on to the skip and peered down inside. His heart froze at the sight that greeted him. There in a scrambled mess lay what, until that very morning, had been the cosy, sweet, and reassuring entrance lobby to his building. Now all that remained of it was a bunch of shattered, hacked, broken, chipped, and splintered scraps of cherry, walnut, and oak.

An armload of spindles crashed on to the pile. Hermux turned back to the beaver, who was chewing the last leg from one of the Windsor chairs that had sat by the window.

'What's going on here?' growled Hermux.

'Boss's orders,' mumbled the beaver through a mouthful of maple chips.

Hermux bent down and retrieved a cluster of carved oak

leaves and acorns that had been part of the moulding around the ceiling.

'Who is this boss?' asked Hermux. 'Who gave him permission to ruin our beautiful lobby? Where is he?'

'Not he, Mr Tantamoq,' said a familiar voice. 'But she. And I am right here.' Tucka Mertslin strode through the doorway dressed in a camouflage canvas jumpsuit, knee-high construction boots, a day-glow orange hard hat, and a utility belt from which hung a tape measure, a walkie-talkie, and a loudhailer. 'And it was you,' she continued full steam, 'you! And all the other little people who live here, who gave me permission to do this. You elected me Chairwoman of the Subcommittee for Hall Decoration. And I am doing my job!'

'We didn't give you permission to ruin the building!' said Hermux.

'Ruin, Mr Tantamoq? I hardly think I've ruined it,' said Tucka in an acid voice. 'I may have saved it from pathetic mediocrity. And I may have rescued it from utter insignificance. But I haven't ruined anything. There was nothing here to ruin.'

'No?' asked Hermux in exasperation. 'What about the lovely old panelling? What about our comfy chairs? What about the handsome paintings of the apple, the pear, the pineapple, and the grapes?'

'Excuse me!' grunted someone behind Hermux. 'Coming through!'

Another beaver staggered out of the building carrying a load of paintings. Or what had been paintings. The frames were smashed at all the corners. And the canvases were ripped and torn exactly as if somebody wearing large construction boots had stomped a foot through each one.

With a great heave the beaver tossed them up into the skip. As they fell from sight, Hermux glimpsed painted fragments of fruit.

'Those paintings have been hanging in this building since before my grandfather's time!' screamed Hermux in outrage.

'Well then, you've proved my point,' said Tucka. 'It's time for a change.'

A loud squawk issued from her walkie-talkie. 'Tucka!' snapped a man's voice. 'You're needed inside. Pronto!'

'I'm on my way!' she shouted into the walkie-talkie.

'Come see what we've done inside,' she urged Hermux as she rushed away. 'And then tell me it's not an improvement! It's too wonderful! I've outdone myself. I really have!'

Chapter 10
A Lesson in History

Hermux stepped cautiously through the front door into the darkened hallway. He felt his way carefully down the steps and slowly back towards the lobby, stepping over loose boards and chunks of fallen plaster.

The lobby was a scene of total chaos. Sheets of plywood had been nailed across the windows overlooking the little courtyard garden. The burnished oak panelling had been stripped away to bare bricks and cement. Sheets of black plastic covered the ceiling. And where the copper chandelier with its amber-lit pine cones had hung, there was now a single lightbulb hanging from a bare wire.

Tucka stood talking with a tall, slender young otter dressed in tight-fitting black leather. They were watching a team of squirrels standing on the tops of tall ladders struggling with big coils of razor-sharp barbed wire. Lengths of the wire were strung along the walls and back and forth across the ceiling.

The otter grabbed the loudhailer from Tucka's belt. 'Gracefully, you bushy-tailed idiots!' he yelled. 'Don't pull it so tight. I want it draped, not stretched. It should feel voluptuous!'

The squirrels leaned out precariously from their ladders, letting the barbed wire fall into big looping spirals.

'Much better!' said the otter. 'Nail it! Now, Tucka! This is your big moment! Here! On the floor by the windows!'

Tucka lay down on the floor and then slowly she began to writhe about as though she'd been struck by a car.

She peered up at the otter while he pranced around encouraging and directing her. 'Yes! Yes!' he said. 'More to the right! Raise your left arm! Twist on to your side! That's it! Bend the knee. Hold it! Right there!'

He knelt beside her and quickly began to trace the outline of her body on to the floor with an enormous stick of chalk. 'This is perfect!' he told her. 'Pure inspiration! Tucka, you're simply marvellous!'

'You bring out my wild side, Rink!' she giggled breathlessly.

When he'd finished tracing, Rink helped Tucka to her feet and dusted the plaster dust from her jumpsuit. Then he snapped his fingers impatiently. 'Squeezle!' he said. 'The handbag!'

A rather nervous-looking chipmunk in a baggy sports jacket ran forward and handed Rink a large lady's handbag.

Rink opened the handbag and dumped the contents on to the floor next to Tucka's outline. There was a tube of lipstick, a comb, a mirror, a wallet, an address book, a ring of keys, a handkerchief, and some loose change. Then he tossed the handbag on the floor and began to jump up and down on it, shouting gleefully, 'My art's the smartest! My art's the smartest!'

After a moment he stopped suddenly and bowed to Tucka. 'Give it a try, love,' he told her.

Tucka leaped into in the air and landed square on the handbag with both boots. 'Hoooeeey,' she howled and ground the handbag under her feet. 'For beauty! For youth! For everything I am!'

'Well, that's a wrap,' Rink told Tucka when she'd exhausted herself. 'Quite a day's work, I'd say.' He nodded curtly to the chipmunk, who set to work roping off the area around the outline and the handbag with yellow plastic tape that said CRIME SCENE in bold letters.

Hermux stood gaping in amazement at the whole spectacle.

'Impressive, isn't it?' said a voice beside him.

'What?' said Hermux, startled out his state of shock.

'I said, "It's impressive, isn't it?" Rink's vision and daring.' A dapper mole with unusually large teeth stepped forward and extended his paw. 'Pup Schoonagliffen,' he said with a friendly grin. 'Design reporter for the *Daily Sentinel*. And you are?'

'Hermux Tantamoq,' said Hermux. 'Watchmaker.'

'Yes. The watchmaker,' said Pup. 'I've seen your shop. Well, what do you think?'

'Think? I don't know what to think yet,' confessed Hermux. 'What are they doing?'

'They're making history. I've followed Rink Firsheen's career from the very beginning when he was doing window displays for Tamintha Bambadini downtown,' explained Pup. 'Now he's Tucka Mertslin's protégé. And this, I believe, will be one of the masterworks we remember him for. The lobby as urban metaphor. Connecting the viewer to the violence of life in the underbelly of the great city.'

'Well put, Pup,' said Rink, joining them. 'You've caught the feeling all right.'

'But when does all this come down?' asked Hermux.

'Come down?' repeated Pup, who sounded surprised.

'COME DOWN?' repeated Rink, who sounded even more surprised.

'COME DOWN?' repeated Tucka, who sounded much more than surprised and whose eyes had turned an ominous shade of red.

'Yes,' said Hermux, pointing at the black plastic, the bare lightbulb, the barbed wire, and the police tape. 'When does all this junk come down? And when does the decoration go up?'

Rink stepped very close to Hermux. He slid his dark glasses down his nose, leaned down, and stared deeply into Hermux's eyes. 'This doesn't come down, my little friend,' he said in a velvety voice. 'This, as you call it, is the decoration.'

He motioned to Tucka. 'Tucka, dear, who is this small fellow?' he asked in a smooth, even more velvety voice.

'This,' said Tucka disdainfully, 'is Mr Hermux Tantamoq. Watchmaker.'

'And may I ask,' said Rink, the velvet in his voice gradually giving way to an ear-splitting shriek that echoed throughout the lobby, 'what does a watchmaker have to do with my changing the course of interior design history?!'

'Nothing, Rink,' Tucka assured him nervously as she led him away by the arm. She cast Hermux a withering look. 'Nothing whatsoever.'

At first Hermux was too astonished to move. Then he

gathered himself together and began to pick his way through the rubble underfoot towards the elevator. Pup Schoonagliffen walked beside him, explaining in a rapturous voice, 'It's revolutionary, Mr Tantamoq. Interior space stripped of sentiment and pretence. Embracing the danger and the filth of street life itself. You're a fortunate mouse, Mr Tantamoq. To be a part of all this.'

'Fortunate?' asked Hermux, somewhat dazed.

'Indeed! Most assuredly. Before you go, Mr Tantamoq, here's my card,' offered Pup cheerfully. 'Perhaps we'll speak again ...'

'Perhaps we should,' answered Hermux, stepping into the elevator. 'My sense of beauty, what there is of it, seems to have fallen out of step.'

'Incidentally, Mr Tantamoq!' boomed Tucka through her loudhailer from across the lobby. 'You must schedule a meeting of the treasury committee immediately! The budget you gave me has proven woefully inadequate for the job. Beauty doesn't come cheaply, Mr Tantamoq. It doesn't come cheaply!'

Chapter 11
A QUESTION OF BEAUTY

'Tell me the truth, Mirrin,' said Hermux, closing the book from which he had been reading aloud. 'Do you think I have a sense of beauty?'

His elderly friend sipped her tea thoughtfully. 'You, Hermux? A sense of beauty?' she asked. 'What an odd question. Well, I would have to say that you do. Not an extravagant one, mind you. But yes. A sense of beauty.'

They sat together on Mirrin's sun porch just off her studio. It overlooked her garden, which was finally beginning to show the faintest signs of approaching spring. 'For example, the way you described for me the little yellow primroses blooming along the path,' she continued. 'Quite accurately, I thought. I could almost see them again.' She smiled. 'Why the sudden concern?'

'I was recently told that I'm limited and narrow,' answered Hermux. 'That I just don't get it. And on top of that, I have no sense of beauty whatsoever.'

'Well, you have one. It's just not the flaming-torch sort, that's all. Yours is more like a candle in a window on an autumn evening.'

'You mean it's dim,' said Hermux, disappointed.

'Who's put this nonsense in your head?' demanded Mirrin.

'Tucka, my neighbour. Tucka Mertslin.'

'Tucka Mertslin? The cosmetics tycoon? You're joking!'

'No. I'm not joking. And neither is she,' he answered. 'To her I'm just an ignorant little rodent who stands in the way of beauty's progress.'

'She was always a conceited little imp!'

'You know her?'

'I taught her. Years ago. At the Art School. Tucka Mertslin. She was certainly talented. And headstrong. And ambitious. And impatient!' laughed Mirrin. 'I'm afraid we didn't get along very well. Well, she's certainly shown us all. Whatever does she look like now?'

Hermux tried his best to convey what details he could about Tucka's hats, her clothes, her shoes, her make-up.

'Stop it, Hermux! You're making this up!'

'I am not!' he exclaimed. 'I'm probably leaving things out!'

'But Hermux, why on earth do you care what Tucka thinks of you? She's not your type.'

'No,' he admitted. 'She's not. But there is someone ... '

'Someone whose opinion of you matters more?' asked Mirrin. 'And who might this someone be?'

So Hermux told her about meeting Ms Perflinger. About Ms Perflinger's heroic rescue flight. About repairing her broken watch. And her failure to return for it.

'She is simply the most dashing and daring mouse on earth!' he finished.

'And you are wondering,' mused Mirrin, 'if she could possibly entertain the notion of life with a quiet, thoughtful watchmaker who has not had perhaps so many adventures, and who may not have the most highly developed sense of beauty?'

'Yes,' agreed Hermux. 'That's it in a nutshell.'

'I see. Then it's serious.' She thought for a moment. 'Well, here's a suggestion. Go over to my bookshelves behind my worktable. And on the second shelf at the very end you should find a small sketchbook. Bring that to me, will you?'

Hermux brought her the sketchbook. 'Now open it up and tell me what's in it,' she instructed him. 'I think I'd only started it when ...' She stopped. 'When ...' she tried again. 'When ...' She let out a dry sob and then caught herself. Hermux gently put his paw on her frail shoulder.

'Oh. I'll be all right,' she apologized. She took a deep breath. 'It's just that sometimes it surprises me like that. I miss seeing. I miss drawing and painting! It's like having the very dearest friend move away and never return.'

Hermux nodded. It hurt him to see her unhappy. As it hurt him to see her studio lifeless and unused these last three years. Unfinished canvases stacked against the wall. Paints on the palette dried and caked. Cans of brushes gathering dust.

Mirrin's blindness was something she rarely mentioned.

She wiped her eyes. 'Now then,' she said firmly. 'What I suggest is that you take this sketchbook. It would make me very happy if you would. I want you to use it as a notebook. And I want you to note things that you see. Like the primroses. You'll be my eyes in the outside world. And you'll read to me about what you've seen. And you will develop your sense of beauty by paying attention to the world around you.'

Hermux took the sketchbook. He ran his paw over its

smooth cover and looked out into the garden, unable to say a word.

'And now, let's not drive ourselves into a funk. I have a surprise!' Mirrin announced brightly. 'I've been given two tickets to *The Gypsy Moth* for tonight at the Opera. Briddy Van Der Larken and Conko di Claramoor. It's completely sold out. You'll be my escort. And together we shall make a dazzling appearance.'

Chapter 12
HIGH DRAMA

As he and Mirrin threaded their way through the crowded lobby and up the grand staircase, Hermux was glad that he had taken special care getting dressed. He wore his dark grey suit, a robin's-egg-blue vest, and his lucky Terfle tie, a silk bow tie printed all over with red and black ladybirds. He had carefully waxed his whiskers, which stood out grandly and perfectly straight. Walking confidently beside him, Mirrin looked quite radiant in a simple black satin gown that set off her silvery fur. Her dark glasses only added to her dramatic appearance.

Everyone seemed drawn to Mirrin. Heads turned to watch as she and Hermux passed by. Mirrin had been right. They were making a dazzling appearance.

'Of course,' thought Hermux. 'I'm the one who is most dazzled.'

'It's marvellous to be out, Hermux,' she told him, squeezing his arm pleasantly. 'I love all the motion, the noise, and the excitement in the air.'

They settled into their seats, and Hermux opened his programme and began to read.

Boskus Todgerleakun's
The Gypsy Moth
An Opera in Three Acts

Libretto
by
Peer Smillendin

The Cast
(in order of vocal appearance)

Kathë the Gypsy Moth	Briddy Van Der Larken
King of the Forest	Erb Brogh
The Messenger	Terlee Parletto
The Warrior Slash	Conko di Claramoor

Pinchester Opera Orchestra & Chorus
Conducted by
Trubby Tolkstottin

Original Production Devised and Directed by
Rink Firsheen

This production was underwritten
by a generous grant from
Tucka Mertslin Cosmetics

Act I
The Forest

Fleeing her murderous lover, Kathë the Gypsy Moth has been blown into the forest by a terrific storm. Her wings are injured, and she is unable to fly further. She resigns herself to life as a lonely exile in the dark forest.

Act II
The Castle of the King

The forest dwellers implore the King to save them from the Gypsy Moth who is devouring the trees. Standing by the Eternal Flame that symbolizes the life force of the forest, the King dispatches the Messenger to find the Warrior Slash and command him to return from his pilgrimage and destroy the Gypsy Moth.

Act III
The Dying Forest

The Warrior Slash has tracked the Gypsy Moth to her lair high in the forest. As he prepares to slay her, she spreads her newly healed wings in terror. He is overcome by her beauty and renounces his loyalty to the King. Kathë and Slash declare their undying love for each other. Slash falls into an exhausted sleep. Knowing that his betrayal of the King will mean his execution, the Gypsy Moth slips away and flies to her death in the Eternal Flame.

'It's a very dramatic story,' whispered Hermux to Mirrin as the chandeliers began to dim and were hoisted towards the ceiling.

'It's preposterous really, but I cry every time I hear it,' said Mirrin. 'I'll never forget seeing Camia Mallis do it. But I hear that Van Der Larken's singing is sublime.'

There was a commotion in one of the large private boxes at the side.

'You're on my foot!' someone hissed.

'Sit down!' snarled someone.

There was much scraping of chairs and rustling of programmes.

'Sssshhhh!'

Through the dark still air of the theatre the unmistakable scent of Tucka Mertslin's perfume drifted like the wash of an ocean liner lapping against a pier.

As the curtain rose and the stage lights came up, Hermux could see her clearly. She was seated next to Rink, fanning herself rather noisily with an enormous parrot-feather fan. A cloud of wires bristled from her head. From each wire hung a golden musical note that bobbed and jiggled as she moved her head in time with the orchestra.

Chapter 13
A Glittering Occasion

The towering forest groaned under the fury of the storm. Angry black clouds raged against a hopeless sky. Suddenly a spotlight pierced the gloom. And the tattered figure of a gypsy moth fluttered into view. Crashing perilously through the tangled trees, she plummeted through the air and stopped her fall only inches above the stage.

A thunder of applause greeted her entrance. She turned majestically to the audience, extended her torn wings slowly, and began to sing:

Driven through darkness by amorous death ...

Her voice, piercing and powerful, soared above the orchestra and swept across the theatre. Hermux's ears twitched. His whiskers jiggled. He sat up and focused his opera glasses on the remarkable figure of Briddy Van Der Larken.

Even as larks go, Briddy was plump. And she was no longer young. But she transformed herself for the role, conveying both the strength and the fragility of the tragic moth. And her voice was, as Mirrin had predicted, sublime.

'As pure as falling water,' thought Hermux. 'Or sunlight. Or a winter night.'

By the time the curtain fell on Act I, Hermux was ecstatic.

'I see what you mean about it,' he told Mirrin as they walked towards the lobby. 'It's captivating.'

'It's only beginning, Hermux. It keeps building right up to the end,' said Mirrin. 'I'm glad you're enjoying it. It's one of my favourites.'

The lobby was buzzing with talk. Groups of people stood arguing with drinks in their hands.

By the time Hermux got Mirrin situated in a comfortable chair and returned with punch, opinions were ricocheting in all directions.

'Briddy's got too fat for the part.'

'Nonsense. She looks stupendous.'

'She's too old. It's time for her to move over for the younger singers.'

'That's ridiculous. She's at her prime. No one has her musicality.'

'The voice is good. I'll grant that. But she can't act. Even at the end, with her voice nearly gone, Mallis was more electric. She was the Moth!'

'I thought she was wonderful,' Hermux confided to Mirrin. 'But maybe I was wrong.'

'She was wonderful,' Mirrin assured him. 'This is the sporting aspect of opera–taking a definite position and defending it. It keeps the adrenaline up during intermission.'

Hermux looked up to see a tall, elegant mouse approaching them. She stopped and smiled. She spoke in a low pleasant voice. 'Mirrin Stentrill, how pleasant to have you with us. It's Ortolina Perriflot.'

'Ortolina,' responded Mirrin, turning towards her. 'How are you?'

'Too busy, of course. I seem to be on every board in creation. But things are about to change. With Father gone, I've taken on the work at the Institute.'

'I was so sorry to hear about him. How are you managing?'

'Well, I miss him, the old devil. I guess I always will. But I'm carrying on. And you, Mirrin. How are you doing?'

'Oh, I manage to keep busy,' she reassured her. 'My friends visit and I try to get out for music. Oh!' she said. 'Forgive me. This is my dear friend Hermux Tantamoq, the watchmaker. Hermux is discovering a new interest in opera.'

'Pleased to make your acquaintance, Mr Tantamoq,' said Ortolina. 'No. Please don't get up. I must run anyway. I've got to congratulate Tucka and Rink. They've done a wonderful job. I had my doubts about both of them. But it's a beautiful production. I'll call you,' she told Mirrin. 'I still haven't given up on the idea of your retrospective at the museum. Goodbye, Mr Tantamoq. Try to convince her that a show would be good for her. And for us.'

Ortolina strode away, her striking head of golden fur visible above much of the crowd.

'A show at the museum?' asked Hermux.

'Yes,' said Mirrin. 'Ten years ago I would have been thrilled. But I'm not now. Too much like my own funeral. I just can't face it. And I can't face the pity. A little pity now and then is rather reassuring. But a lot of it? All at once? It's suffocating.'

Mirrin was clearly upset. Hermux sensed that she might want to be alone for a moment so he excused himself and went to get them each some more punch. Standing in line, he marvelled at the energy of the colourful crowd and tried to note the details of what he was seeing as Mirrin had suggested.

'Glamorous, isn't it?'

Hermux turned to find Pup Schoonagliffen beside him, grinning his toothy grin, notebook in hand.

'It's wonderful,' said Hermux. 'I haven't been much before.'

'Oh, she's in rare voice all right. Bit chunky, though. Look for my review tomorrow. Of course she's not Mallis. But then who is? Even Mallis wasn't Mallis for very long.

'Who's your friend there?' asked Pup, changing the subject.

'Mirrin Stentrill, the painter.'

'Ah, yes. The painter. I've seen her work. Never would have guessed she was blind. A blind painter. Now there's a story.'

'Well, she doesn't paint any more. So she's not a blind painter. She's a painter who went blind. And she's a very private person besides,' Hermux said protectively.

'Take it easy, old mouse, I'm just fulfilling my newsgathering responsibilities as Arts Reporter. Listen, Tantamoq, you seem to be right in the thick of things. I'm thinking of writing a profile of you. I see you as a sort of Everymouse standing at the edge of Art and asking, 'What does it all mean?' That sort of thing.

Naturally I'll need my editor's approval. But give it some thought, will you? There's Tucka and Rink now. I've got to interview them. I'll catch you later.'

And he was gone.

When Hermux made it back to Mirrin, he found her surrounded by a small crowd. Tucka Mertslin was wedged into the seat next to Mirrin smiling benevolently and gesturing dramatically with her fan. Pup Schoonagliffen was directing questions at the two of them.

'And you haven't seen each other since then?' he asked.

'No. After Miss Stentrill banned me from her class, I left the Art School. In fact I suppose I owe quite a lot of my phenomenal success to her. Otherwise I might have ended up as just another boring old painter with a house full of unsold canvases.'

Hermux saw Mirrin wince.

'Not that that's what you are, dear,' Tucka continued innocently. 'But you know what I mean. I just saw things on a bigger scale, that's all. Ah, Mr Tantamoq! The very mouse I was looking for!'

'Me?' sputtered Hermux, nearly dropping the two cups of punch.

'Yes,' she said with sudden sweetness. 'I wonder if I could trouble you to come to my office tomorrow morning on a matter of considerable urgency.'

The crowd turned to Hermux expectantly.

'I ... I ... I am sure I would be delighted,' he acquiesced gloomily.

'It's the budget for the hall,' he thought drearily. 'It must be a whopper.'

'Fine,' said Tucka decisively, making the swarm of musical notes above her head vibrate wildly. 'Ten a.m. sharp. And now I must excuse myself. Let's not hold up the curtain.'

And within moments they were all returning to their seats.

Chapter 14
THE CASE OF THE VANISHING FOREST

After the passion and desperation of Act I, Hermux thought Act II was a bit of a letdown.

A procession of forest folk arrived at the castle gate and slowly (a little too slowly) made their way up the steps to beg an audience with the King. Then the King and the Queen, and the princes and princesses, and the prime minister, and the assistant prime minister, and the ladies in waiting, and the noble knights, and a large group of unidentified hangers-on (each of whom seemed to have something to say about the situation) descended from within the castle.

Then the spokes-toad for the Forest Folk stepped forward and explained that Kathë the Gypsy Moth was devouring the entire forest canopy. Soon it would be gone. And when that happened they would all perish. The implication of course was that the King and his court would be short-staffed soon thereafter.

Then a large drum began booming and a band of hooded figures marched on and surrounded the King. 'Another parade,' thought Hermux, who was not overly fond of parades. 'Must be the Forest Inquisitors.'

Then a heated argument broke out among the Forest Folk, the Forest Inquisitors, and the members of the court about what was to be done.

Hermux found his mind wandering back to the intermission. 'Imagine,' he thought. 'I met Ortolina Perriflot, the richest woman in the world. And she was nicer than I would have thought. And I may be interviewed for a newspaper article.' Hermux checked back at the stage. The argument was heating up. And it seemed like the Eternal Flame was getting bigger. He opened his programme very quietly and leafed through it in the near darkness.

It looked like there was a big photograph of Tucka Mertslin in the back. At least it resembled Tucka. Although in the dark she seemed to look a lot younger.

A cymbal crashed in the orchestra and Hermux looked up. The Forest Folk were all kneeling before the King. The Inquisitors had thrown back their hoods, revealing eerie bone-white masks. The King was handing a huge scroll which was probably Kathë's death warrant to the Messenger, who was played by a very trim-looking woodchuck with a nice baritone voice. The Eternal Flame blazed up, sending ominous shadows dancing across the backdrop. The Messenger exited with a flourish on a high note, and the curtain dropped like a guillotine.

The house lights came up. And Hermux was startled to find an enormous close-up of Tucka Mertslin staring up at him from the programme. She didn't look just younger. She looked positively, radiantly rejuvenated.

```
┌─────────────────────────────────────┐
│ ┌─────────────────────────────────┐ │
│ │                                 │ │
│ │  M I L L E N N I U M            │ │
│ │  THE COUNTDOWN HAS BEGUN.       │ │
│ │                                 │ │
│ │                                 │ │
│ │                                 │ │
│ │  TUCKA MERTSLIN COSMETICS       │ │
│ │  You're only as old as you look!│ │
│ │                                 │ │
│ └─────────────────────────────────┘ │
└─────────────────────────────────────┘
```

Chapter 15
TUCKA SPRINGS A TRAP

'Would you mind if we just stayed here for this intermission?' asked Mirrin. 'I'm not sure I'm ready for another round of surprises.'

'Sure,' said Hermux. 'You know I was really surprised by Ortolina Perriflot. Not what I expected at all. She seemed nice actually.'

'Oh, Ortolina's a pretty good egg. This is her mature period. She's been through a lot.'

'How do you know her?'

'I've known Ortolina since she was a child. I painted her portrait. It was one of my first commissions. She was a miserable little thing. Spoiled in some ways and deprived in others. Didn't like me making her sit still. And what child would really? Anyway I needed the money badly so I forged ahead. And we reached a sort of truce finally. Something to do with my smuggling an endless supply of gummy bears into the house. Perriflot was starting his research on tooth decay then, and she was forbidden to have any sweets. Since then Ortolina and I have been very friendly. But Ortolina isn't someone I'd ever want to cross.'

'And Tucka? What was the story there? What on earth did she do that made you kick her out of your class?'

'Well, Tucka was smart. There was never any question about that. But she was never one for hard work. It was the end of the term, and she had promised me a series of monumental paintings with a social message. But she hadn't shown me anything. Then she vanished. She barricaded herself in her studio and wouldn't let any of us near. It was all very hush-hush.

'Well, you can imagine the anticipation we felt to find out what she was doing in there. And then she posted a sign announcing her showing. And all of us, students and faculty alike, showed up. She had also got the student paper and the city paper to come. Then she opened the door to the studio, and we all trooped in in a mass. Her studio was stripped completely bare. There was a horrible squeaking sound coming from speakers hidden somewhere.

'And there, right in the centre, on a raised platform, brutally lit by a spotlight, stood a hideous, enormous mousetrap. A real one I suppose, though I shudder to think how she got her paws on it. Anyway there it was. Baited with a chunk of livid orange cheese. Like some horrible cartoon. With a small sign, on a prissy little museum stand, that said, *Art is dead. You could be next.*'

'Oh, my goodness,' said Hermux.

'In hindsight it seems like just the sort of silly prank you'd expect in an art school. But at the time it was shocking. Painful. In such poor taste, and really, I thought, diabolical, cruel, and unfeeling. Of course that was probably Tucka's point. In any case, I didn't get it. I overreacted. I screamed. I called her a barbarian. I told her to get out of my class. And the rest is, as Tucka so grandly puts it, history. I can only imagine how much she enjoyed having me there with her in the spotlight tonight. The dear old doddering professor. And blind now, too. Now that's poetic justice. At least for Tucka it is.'

Hermux didn't know what to say.

'Speaking of barbarians,' he ventured. 'That reporter thinks he might want to interview me as a sort of modern-day barbarian. An Everymouse looks at Art. I expect he'll make a fool of me.'

'Why, I think that would be fun, Hermux. Why not? A lot of art is foolish. Perhaps you'll have time to write in your notebook before then.'

'Something tells me that showing Pup my attempts to write about beauty would be a fatal mistake,' mused Hermux. 'Thanks, but I don't think I'll push my luck there.'

Chapter 16
FEELINGS

Mirrin was right about *The Gypsy Moth*. It was preposterous in a way. But when Kathë left the Warrior Slash sleeping in her lair and flew away into the night, Hermux's throat tightened. 'Farewell to life as cruel as death, ' Kathë sang, circling closer and closer to the Eternal Flame. Then she plunged at last to her fiery fate.

Hermux sobbed audibly. Mirrin reached over and squeezed his paw. She took several tissues from her purse and handed one to Hermux.

As the curtain descended and the audience broke into shouts and applause, Hermux wiped his eyes and blew his nose.

They didn't speak much during the taxi ride to Mirrin's house. They were both lost in thought. Hermux walked Mirrin to her door.

'Thank you so much,' said Hermux. 'I had no idea what I was missing. I'll never forget tonight.'

'You're very sweet, Hermux. And you cut a very dashing figure tonight. I can't see you, but I'm sure of it. Good-night.'

Hermux decided to walk back to his apartment. The light rain had stopped, and the soft air carried the rich scents of wet earth and vegetation coming back to life. By the time he crawled into bed he was truly tired. But before he switched off the light he remembered Mirrin's sketchbook. It wouldn't do to miss writing in it the very first day. So he fetched it and a pen from his study and a glass of apple juice from the kitchen, and settled himself against a stack of pillows while he thought back through the day.

At daybreak a tint of rose crept close upon the darkened city, washing away the night and bathing the sleeping buildings in the golden promise of morning ...

'No,' he thought. 'It should probably be "the pink promise of morning".'

He crossed it out and began again.

Night, exhausted at last, released the city from its strangling embrace and slunk away into the west like a rejected lover.

'Now that's more like it,' he thought. 'More vigorous. More to the point. And more ... well, ridiculous, I guess. If I'm going to start with sunrise I guess I'd better get up earlier tomorrow so I can see what it actually looks like.'

He crossed it out.

He sat for a long time without writing anything. He thought back through the day. The visit to Mirrin. Her garden. The opera. Briddy Van Der Larken and Ortolina Perriflot and Tucka Mertslin. He thought about the mousetrap. He thought about a gypsy moth whose wings were russet, amber, crimson and black, flying through darkness towards a golden flame.

'Except for the opera,' thought Hermux, 'it was only an ordinary day in the life of an ordinary watchmaker. But somehow I don't feel ordinary. I feel changed.'

He put his pen to the paper again and wrote slowly and deliberately.

Thank you for friendship most of all. Thank you for cufflinks. And for singing larks dressed up like carnival moths. Thank you for dark theatres. For mousetraps even. Thank you for Terfle. For cotton sheets and soft pillows and apple juice. And cheese.

Then Hermux closed the sketchbook, turned out the light, shut his eyes, and slept.

Chapter 17
A MEETING IN SHANGRI-LA

It was exactly five minutes before ten o'clock when Hermux stepped into the grand lobby of the Tucka Mertslin Empire of Beauty Building. Against his better judgement Hermux was impressed. The floor and the walls were made of pure white marble. The domed ceiling was white and brilliantly lit. Bold letters floated above the surface of the curved wall and clearly identified this as the Tucka Mertslin Empire of Beauty. The letters were also white. Even the uniform of the guard at the reception desk was white. The only visible colour was the monumental vase of red flowers that stood in the centre. Strange tropical flowers with a vaguely carnivorous quality about them.

Conscious that his green plaid suit made him pitifully conspicuous in this relentless field of white, Hermux scurried to the reception desk and told the guard he had an appointment with Ms Mertslin.

The guard telephoned upstairs and then motioned Hermux to the bank of elevators.

'Tenth floor,' he said.

On the tenth floor Hermux was met by a plain-looking mouse in a plain-looking brown suit wearing enormous eyeglasses.

'Mr Tantamoq, I'm Blanda Nergup,' she said. 'Tucka Mertslin's personal assistant. Madame Mertslin is expecting you. Please come with me.'

Although she was quite tall, Blanda Nergup walked with such a pronounced stoop that Hermux, who seldom looked down at anyone, found himself looking down at the back of her head. She had the most peculiar, unruly head of fur. It was coarse and unusually long. Hermux thought she looked very odd. Then he caught himself. 'I'm going to try to keep an open mind,' he told himself. 'She works in the fashion world so she must know what she's doing. It probably just takes some getting used to.' But it did look extremely dry. He remembered what had happened to the Gypsy Moth, and he hoped that Ms Nergup was cautious around open flames.

Blanda threw open the double doors leading to Tucka's private office and waved Hermux inside.

'She'll be with you in a moment.'

Tucka's office glowed like a cloud of pink candyfloss. The carpeting was so thick that Hermux had to lift his feet carefully to keep from getting entangled in the fleecy pile.

Tucka's desk sat on a raised platform in the centre of the office. It resembled a lavish birthday cake iced with white and gold frosting. It was strewn with telephones and papers and coffee cups and brushes and combs and tubes of lipstick and cans of fur spray.

He walked around it to get to the wall of windows and looked out at the gleaming towers of the city. It was what magazines call a commanding view. Tucka was obviously a captain of industry. 'It must be wonderful,' he thought, 'to see the whole world spread before you like this.'

His reverie was interrupted by a shrill voice that seemed to come from the wall behind the desk. There was, Hermux now saw, a small door set into the wall. The door was slightly ajar.

It was Tucka's voice. And not her pleasant voice either. But the other one. Hermux knew the difference now. This was the one that made the short hairs on his tail stand at attention. The one that made him click his teeth together nervously. He wasn't sure he should be hearing this, and he did not want to be caught eavesdropping. He moved away from her desk and went to the far couch where he climbed up and took a seat.

Suddenly Tucka's voice went up a painful octave and a full notch in volume.

'And I tell you, Mennus,' she shouted. 'I've got way too much riding on this for any more delays! The product launch is less than thirty days off. If the formula's not ready in time for it, you won't have to worry about the next mortgage payment on the clinic, because when I'm through with you, you won't be practising medicine. In fact you'll be lucky to be shampooing crickets in a pet store! Do you hear me?' she screamed. There was the sound of a phone being slammed down violently.

Moments later Tucka emerged into the office, scowling and wiping her fingers hastily with a tissue.

Hermux looked at her hands. Her claws appeared to be dripping with blood. He gasped and leapt to his feet, spilling the stack of financial reports he'd brought to demonstrate to Tucka the limited financial resources of their apartment building.

63

'You!' she squeaked nervously.

She crossed quickly to her desk and punched a button on the intercom. 'Nergup!' she barked. 'Get in here!'

'Whatever's happened, Tucka?' Hermux blurted out.

Tucka only glared at Hermux. She grabbed a wad of tissues from her desk and scrubbed violently at her fingers.

Blanda Nergup rushed in out of breath.

'Get Mr Tantamoq a cup of coffee!' shouted Tucka. 'And get rid of those hideous glasses, you imbecile! You're deliberately trying to provoke me!'

Blanda removed her thick glasses with the round plastic frames and, squinting uncomfortably, made her way back towards the door. Tucka vanished back into her dressing-room. And Hermux gathered up his papers and returned to his seat on the couch.

'Madame is experimenting with nail polishes this morning,' explained Blanda as she poured Hermux's coffee. 'She's under a lot of pressure right now. With the launch and all.'

Tucka re-emerged, smiling demurely as though nothing had happened.

'Mr Tantamoq!' she gushed in her pleasant voice. 'How very nice of you to come!'

Hermux nodded. He hesitated to say anything just yet.

'As you must know,' she continued without looking at him, 'I am about to introduce the most revolutionary product in the history of cosmetics. The Millennium Line. Eternal youth in a bottle. Shangri-La, Mr Tantamoq! Nothing less than Shangri-La. A mixture of medicine and cosmetology not seen on this earth since the fabled era of the ancient pharaohs!'

Hermux nodded again as though he understood perfectly.

'But I have run into a little snag.' She paused.

The silence in the room became very oppressive. Hermux shifted his position on the couch.

'It's quite ridiculous really,' she went on. 'But we've run into a packaging problem. I've hired the best designers, the most brilliant minds in the business. But I've got nothing really. Nothing with style. Nothing with presence. Nothing with impact. And then yesterday I was thinking. It's *time* we're dealing with. It's time we're stopping. And that's when I thought of you. Who would know more about time than a watchmaker? And your collection, of course. And then I realized that you, Mr Tantamoq, are the solution. We shall base our packaging on the classic forms of the watch and the clock.'

Hermux continued to nod.

'Tomorrow I shall send my new assistant, the charming Miss Nergup, whom you have met. And she will make a selection of watches and clocks from your collection. And my designers will study them and prepare drawings and moulds to cast our bottles from. And your pieces will become immortal. Naturally you'll be given some sort of credit for your cooperation. Some sort of mention. It needn't be conspicuous, of course, but some sort of identification in the fine print or maybe on the inside of the bottom of the box.'

'Well, I'm not sure really,' Hermux hesitated.

'Why on earth not?' snarled Tucka. 'Do you have any idea how long a mouse lives? Or a squirrel? Or a hamster? Have you any idea how horrible it is to shrivel, to grow old and die? I am going to put a stop to that. And you're not going to stand in my way!'

Then she caught herself and switched back to her pleasant voice. 'And naturally,' she went on very cordially, 'there's absolutely nothing to worry about. Your watches will be exquisitely cared for. Every precaution will be taken to return them in the pristine condition in which we receive them. You needn't worry one bit. This is all standard procedure.'

'Standard procedure?' questioned Hermux.

'Of course,' she reassured him. 'This is done every day. It's absolutely business-as-usual. Don't give it another thought.'

She punched the intercom again. 'Nergup! Now!' she bleated.

Miss Nergup popped her head in the door.

'Mr Tantamoq will see you tomorrow to show you his collection,' she explained genially. She turned back to Hermux. 'What time did you say, Mr Tantamoq?'

'Well, I didn't say actually.'

Tucka glowered at him.

'But I think that the morning would be good. How about eleven o'clock?'

'Splendid! Ms Nergup will be at your shop at eleven o'clock tomorrow. Thank you so much for coming. It has been simply marvellous to spend time with you. But I really must get back to work. Nergup, show Mr Tantamoq out!'

Hermux gathered up his papers. Tucka seemed to have completely forgotten the lobby for the time being. And Hermux had no desire to bring it up.

He rode the elevator back to the lobby and stepped out to find a beehive of activity. A crew of young flying squirrels in white painter's overalls was installing a row of enormous billboards that encircled the lobby. It was the ad of Tucka that had been in the opera programme repeated over and over. It made Hermux a little nervous to see Tucka's face blown up to such enormous proportions and staring at him from every direction. She looked a good bit younger in the pictures than she had just now upstairs. Maybe it was the light.

'Inspiring, isn't it?'

Hermux turned to find Pup Schoonagliffen smiling at him. 'Photographs incredibly well, doesn't she? The woman's a genius! And so is her retoucher ...'

'Hi, Pup! What are you doing here?' asked Hermux.

'I'm covering Health and Beauty. Advance piece on her new cosmetics line,' answered Pup. 'Tucka's a major advertiser. It's my job to build a little excitement. See my review yet from last night? What'd you think?'

'Some of it was a little over my head.'

'Hey, that's okay. It's supposed to be. Just doing my job.'

There was a terrific hammering and then a banner unfurled above the portraits of Tucka.

```
┌─────────────────────────────────────┐
│                                     │
│   M I L L E N N I U M               │
│   THE  COUNTDOWN  HAS  BEGUN.       │
│                                     │
│                                     │
│                                     │
│   Only   ┌──┐  days    left!        │
│          │29│                       │
│   TUCKA  └──┘ MERTSLIN COSMETICS    │
│                                     │
└─────────────────────────────────────┘
```

Chapter 18
BLANDA'S MISSION

Hermux was in a good mood the next day when he opened the shop. The sun was out. The rain clouds had blown away. And he had an interesting day's work ahead of him.

Plowt Sandigrin's great-uncle had died and left him an enormous old cuckoo clock. Plowt's great-uncle had bought it for his wife while they were honeymooning in Grebbenland. It had hung in their dining-room for more than fifty years.

It was unusually elaborate even for a cuckoo clock. The body of the clock was a rustic twig hut with a stone chimney and shuttered windows made of birch bark. The clock was powered by bronze pine-cone weights that hung from long chains. The pendulum was a cuckoo's nest carved with three baby cuckoos who opened their beaks and begged for food as the mother bird called out the hours up above. Two squirrels perched on the roof of the little house and scolded noisily at the half-hour.

The face of the clock showed the phases of the moon. The clock had arrived packed in a massive wooden crate. Plowt had unpacked it himself, hung it and wound it by pulling the bronze pine cones on long chains.

After a moment of encouraging whirring sounds, the cuckoo's door had sprung open. The cuckoo had emerged and let out a squawk. The squirrels had begun their scolding. The baby cuckoos had commenced begging. It was all a terrific racket. 'Rather magnificent!' Plowt had called it.

But the racket didn't stop with that. The cuckoo kept right on squawking. And it must be said that its voice left something to be desired in the area of sweetness. The squirrels kept up their scolding. The baby birds continued begging. And then the chime started in clanging mightily.

That's when Plowt got nervous and started looking for a switch to shut it off. But there was no switch. Little Plowt Jr began to wail pitifully. Mrs Sandigrin covered her ears and began to shout at the top of her voice, 'Turn it off, Plowt! Turn it off!'

But Plowt couldn't make out what she was saying because the cuckoo had started whistling the love duet from *The Gypsy Moth*. And the squirrels had begun to pelt him with carved wooden acorns. And that hurt!

Finally in desperation Plowt had grabbed the end of both chains and yanked them as hard as he could. The clock lurched to a halt with a most sickening thwang! The cuckoo stopped whistling and just stood there staring blankly from its perch. The baby birds left off begging and sat dumbly, glassy-eyed, with their beaks open to the ceiling. The squirrels stopped tossing acorns and glared mutely, with their tails puffed and arched magnificently over their backs.

That's when Plowt had called Hermux. And that's why the cuckoo clock was partially disassembled on Hermux's

69

work table. And why Hermux's *Encyclopedia of Cuckoo Clocks and Their Makers* lay open on his desk.

After weeks of over-wound pocket watches and under-wound wristwatches, Hermux was looking forward to sinking his teeth into a good gnarly cuckoo clock.

He had managed to dismantle the two squirrels' heads and was studying the drive mechanism that made their tails twitch when the shop door opened and Ms Nergup stepped in.

'Good morning, Mr Tantamoq! Thank you so much for seeing me.'

Away from Tucka Mertslin's Empire of Beauty, she seemed much brighter and less stooped.

'Good morning, Ms Nergup,' said Hermux pleasantly. She really did have the oddest fur-do. Today it was all swept over to one side, where it sprang out from her head in two bulky braids. She wore long bangs that nearly obscured her eyes.

'Do you mind if I put these on?' she asked, taking her enormous eyeglasses out from her purse. 'Tucka won't let me wear them around her, but I'm absolutely blind without them.'

'Of course I don't mind,' said Hermux. 'You're here to see the collection. So you'd better see it.'

Hermux crossed to the safe and, fitting the small gold key to the lock, he opened the heavy door and swung it back.

'What in particular are you hoping to find?'

'Something marvellous, I hope. Or I'm afraid I'll be fired. Madame Mertslin is very demanding to work for. I'm terrified that I'll disappoint her. And this job means so much to me.'

Hermux slipped a black velvet tray from its slot, set it on the counter, and adjusted the light to shine directly on it.

'These are quite marvellous seventeenth-century pendant watches. The decoration is enamel on gold. This one has a map of the Western Empire. Look, it even shows dragons swimming in the sea.'

'It's beautiful,' said Blanda.

'This one is silver. Simpler and more modern. It's a very early railroad watch. Nineteenth-century. The train is embossed on the side. Beneath a crescent moon.'

Hermux showed her necklace watches, musical watches, pocket watches, watches hidden in the heads of canes, watches set in the handles of daggers. He showed her clocks. Clocks that showed the movement of planets and stars, clocks that showed the movement of the tides, clocks in lanterns, travel clocks in jewel-covered folding cases, and skeleton clocks that had no cases at all.

After an hour he stopped.

'This is a remarkable collection, Mr Tantamoq. I feel honoured to have seen them. They're astonishing. And there are several that will be wonderful for the Millennium foundation, the fur-glow, and mood-shadow. But our first product is the Millennium Elixir. It's a liquid that is taken internally. At least that's what I've been told so far. So the container must work as a bottle, you see.'

'Ah,' said Hermux. 'A bottle. Then perhaps I have an idea.' He reached deep into the safe and withdrew a black leather box which he sat carefully on the counter. He opened the catch on the lid and folded back the side panels. Inside was a beautiful hourglass of blown crystal set in a framework of engraved gold.

'It's magnificent!' gasped Ms Nergup. 'Just magnificent.'

71

'This was made by my great-great-great-great-great-grandfather. Do you think it will do?'

'It will do beautifully,' said Ms Nergup. 'Madame Mertslin will love it. It says *time* perfectly.'

'Of course you'll take good care of it.'

'Very good care. I assure you,' said Ms Nergup. 'We'll return it in perfect condition.'

'Exactly what will they do with it?' asked Hermux.

'Well, I expect they'll make a mould of it. And then they'll refine it. Of course they'll have to work out the opening and the stopper. But the form and the scale are perfect as they are. I'm sure of that.'

'It's all rather exciting, isn't it?' said Hermux. 'It will be seen around the world.'

'It will be seen and touched around the world,' assured Ms Nergup. 'I think your great-great-great-great-great-grandfather would be very proud.'

'I'm rather proud myself,' confided Hermux.

Chapter 19
MECHANICAL INCLINATIONS

After Ms Nergup departed carrying the carefully wrapped hourglass, Hermux returned to the cuckoo clock. He straightened out the kinks in the squirrels' drive shaft. That was simple enough. Then he removed the back of the clock and began to examine the timing mechanism that controlled the cuckoo, the baby birds, the squirrels, and the chime. This was a small metal drum with teeth set in a complicated pattern. When the drum revolved, each of the teeth moved a small rod or a ratchet, and these controlled the motions of the clock figures. Many of the teeth were worn down, and some were missing entirely. The clock was even older than Hermux had initially thought.

Hermux did a detailed drawing of the drum and the teeth. He measured the teeth with tiny calipers and was about to begin cutting new teeth from a sheet of brass when the shop door opened again.

'Oh, Mr Tantamoq! I'm so relieved that you're here.' It was Cladenda Noddem. 'I'm afraid Nock has really made a mess of things.'

Hermux came out from his workroom. 'Well. What's he done now?' he asked.

'He's been crimping pennies in the gears of grandfather's clock. And now he's got one jammed. And the clock has stopped entirely. And I'm afraid he may have ruined it completely this time. I'm at my wit's end with that boy.'

'Well, now, maybe things aren't as bad as all that. Pennies, huh? Whatever for?'

'He's been selling them to the children at school. Crimped pennies for five cents a piece. He says he's made five dollars. And I say that he'll spend every penny of that fixing the clock.'

'Why don't I come out to your house this time? It's not good for that clock to keep moving it.'

'Oh, that would be very kind of you, Mr Tantamoq.'

'I should be done with this cuckoo clock of Plowt Sandigrin's by tomorrow. Barring any surprises. Why don't I come out the day after tomorrow? I'll call you and set up a time. And I think we might want to consider a new hobby for Nock. Something mechanical perhaps. But having to do with something besides clocks.'

Hermux had no sooner returned to the cuckoo clock than the bell on the front door jingled again. 'Did you forget something?' he asked without looking up from his workbench.

'No. I forgot nothing,' replied a sour voice.

Hermux raised his head. A tall grey rat with a long narrow face leaned over the counter and reached with long skinny claws towards the 'Will Call' shelf.

'I've come for Linka Perflinger's watch,' he said with an unpleasant smile.

Chapter 20
FOLLOW THAT RAT!

'Ah yes, Ms Perflinger,' said Hermux, stepping out of his workroom. 'And where is Ms Perflinger?'

'I don't think that's any of your concern,' replied the rat.

'No. Perhaps it isn't. And you would be?'

'Ms Perflinger's representative,' said the rat, licking his thin lips with his sharp tongue. 'Ms Perflinger is out of the country on assignment.'

'May I have the claim ticket, please?'

'I don't have it with me,' said the rat testily.

'Well, this is very irregular. I'm afraid I can't release the watch to a complete stranger without the claim check.'

'Take a bit of free advice, friend,' said the rat in a distinctly unfriendly voice. 'Give me the watch and be done with it.' He leaned forward over the counter, towering over Hermux.

Hermux braced himself, stood up as straight as he could, and looked directly into the rat's shifty yellow eyes.

'I would be more than happy to give you the watch ... if you had the claim ticket. And now I'll give you a bit of free advice. I run an orderly business here. I always have. And claim tickets are an important part of the order. My first loyalty is to my customer, who in this case is Ms Perflinger. I cannot release her watch without a claim ticket. I am very sorry.'

'Listen, mouse,' snapped the rat. 'You've got no idea who you're talking to.'

'Well, I am less and less convinced that I'm talking to any friend of Linka Perflinger. That's for sure. Now, unless you have other business to discuss, I bid you good-day!'

'I'll be back,' said the rat. 'Count on that!'

'I look forward to it. Just bring the claim check with you and a total of twenty-two dollars to cover the repair charges. And you have a watch. Which, I might point out, is still keeping perfect time.'

The rat stomped out of the shop and slammed the door behind him.

Hermux grabbed his hat and coat, scribbled a note to post on the shop door, picked up the morning paper and slipped outside. He was out on the street in moments. The rat was at the north corner just crossing the street. Hermux raised the paper, pretended to read. He turned so he could watch the rat's reflection in the shop window. As soon as the rat was across the intersection, Hermux flipped up his coat collar, pulled his hat down low, and scurried after him.

Hermux was careful to stay well behind the rat. He tried to blend into the traffic on the sidewalk, walking with groups when he could, stopping in front of store windows when he couldn't, crossing to the other side of the street, but always keeping the rat in sight.

The rat was in a hurry. He threaded his way down Ferbosh Avenue past the nice shops, turned right on to

76

Grandle Street and continued past the courthouse, past the tramlines, and headed towards the river. The buildings here were older and stacked closer together. The streets were narrower. It was harder for Hermux to stay out of sight, and he fell behind. At the corner of Grandle and Nickin the rat suddenly disappeared.

Hermux rushed forward. A tall, dingy fortress of a building–the Progressive Tower–occupied the corner. Its brass revolving door was still spinning slowly. Hermux hesitated a moment and then pushed his way inside.

The lobby was completely empty. The doors of one of the four elevators clanged shut. Hermux scooted across the gleaming terrazzo, watching the hand above the elevator as it slowly climbed to the twenty-sixth floor. He punched the UP button and waited impatiently.

Hermux studied the bronze relief map that covered the wall at the end of the lobby. It showed the Western Hemisphere. Pinchester was clearly marked at the top of the map with a large star. Hermux followed the river that ran west through the mountains and out to the vast wheatlands. He traced the railroad south along the curving coastline to the pine forests. He studied the Gulf of Tretch and its crisscrossed steamship lines. Far across its emptiness he gazed at the rugged coastline of Teulabonari, wondering if Ms Perflinger was possibly there at that very moment. And whether she was in some sort of trouble.

A bell rang, and the elevator doors opened. Hermux stepped in quickly and punched the glowing button for the twenty-sixth floor. The elevator rose fast. Hermux braced himself against the sudden upward force, and when the elevator stopped at twenty-six he flew several inches up into the air. Hermux staggered off uncertainly. The dimly lit hallway stretched away into the distance. There were more than a dozen doors. But there was no sign of the rat.

Cautiously Hermux began to explore. He stopped at the door to the first office. Painted in black letters on the frosted glass it said, Abacus Instruction and Rentals. Hermux listened carefully at the door. There was no sound.

Next to that was Accordion Repairs. Inside Hermux could hear the melancholy sound of someone playing a wheezy tango on an accordion that was slightly out of tune.

Muffled screams were audible behind the door marked Amusement Park Personnel. A handwritten note listed immediate openings for a Haunted House Attendant and a Roller Coaster Operator.

Inside the next office Hermux thought he could hear someone playing a rather mournful one-handed tune on a piano. The sign on the door said Artificial Paws—New & Used.

After that came Ash and Hairball Removal. Then the Association of Monotonous Therapy. Hermux listened carefully. Someone was talking in a very low voice. But Hermux couldn't make out anything that was being said.

Then the Astral Projection Club, Atlases—Antique & Modern, Attic Maintenance & Supplies, Austerity Seminars, Automated Laboratory Equipment, and finally Aviators Anonymous.

'That must be it!' thought Hermux. 'It's something to do with Ms Perflinger.' He stepped stealthily to the door and pressed his ear to the glass.

Suddenly the door across the hall opened. It was the rat!

'Fine!' he was saying to someone inside the Automated Laboratory Equipment office. 'Get it assembled and deliver it to Dr Mennus as soon as possible. Send it directly to the clinic.'

Before the rat turned and saw him, Hermux twisted the Aviators Anonymous doorknob and launched himself through the door and nearly into the lap of the startled receptionist inside.

'Mr Dingly?' she asked in surprise.

'No,' said an embarrassed Hermux. 'I'm Mr Tantamoq.'

'Do you have an appointment?' she inquired, suddenly suspicious.

'Well, yes,' stuttered Hermux. 'Or rather, no. Actually I had an appointment. Or rather I have an appointment. But I'm afraid it's someplace else. And I'm terribly late.'

He jumped back to the door, opened it a crack and peered out into the hallway. The rat was gone.

'I'll call to re-schedule,' Hermux told the perplexed receptionist. 'Thank you so much!' And tipping his hat politely, Hermux raced away towards the elevators.

By the time he reached the lobby the rat was gone again. Hermux ran out through the revolving doors and caught sight of the rat walking back through the rush-hour crowds towards the tram. Hermux ran after him.

He caught up with him on the passenger platform just as the Number 3 tram rolled to a stop. Hermux pushed his way into the last car and grabbed a seat by the window. The rat got into the car in front of him.

Hermux opened the newspaper and raised it to cover his

face. Periodically he lowered it just enough to keep an eye on the rat.

After six stops the rat pulled the stop cord and got up to leave. Hermux raised his paper. At the last possible moment he jumped up and bolted for the door. Outside Hermux found himself on the pavement in front of a neighbourhood grocery store. As the trolley pulled away, Hermux spotted the rat walking with a very determined stride down a twisty narrow street lined with small houses. Hermux gave him a head start and then followed.

The streetlights were just coming on. And in the amber light Hermux could make out the white type on the street sign at the corner.

PICKDORNDLE LANE
REALLY FRIENDLY STREET. REALLY FRIENDLY NEIGHBOURS.
NO THROUGH ROAD.

Chapter 21
STAKEOUT

'What is that rat doing on Ms Perflinger's street?' wondered Hermux. 'What if they really are friends? That would be awful. But what if they aren't? That could be even worse.'

He slipped into the shadow of a laurel hedge where he could survey Pickdorndle Lane without being seen. It was a short street that came to a dead-end at the park. The rat crossed over to the other side of the street. He stopped midway, looked back towards Hermux, and studied the scene carefully. Hermux held his breath.

'He obviously doesn't want to be followed,' thought Hermux. 'I wonder if I'm quite the right mouse for this job.'

The rat scurried forward, opened the gate, and vanished up the walk of the next to last house.

'Well, no matter now,' sighed Hermux. 'I'm the only one that seems to have applied.'

Hermux tried to think what he would do if the rat caught him spying on him. He did seem like a nasty character. And he had threatened Hermux at the shop. Hermux looked at the other houses. Maybe the neighbours were friendly like the street sign said, but they were nowhere to be seen.

Hermux took a deep breath and moved as silently as a phantom down the darkening street.

Luckily for him, there was a large rhododendron bush in the front yard of the house directly across the street from Number 3–the house the rat had entered. Hermux crawled inside the rhododendron and situated himself to wait and see what happened next.

He didn't have to wait very long. A light came on in the front room upstairs. The blind was pulled, but clearly etched on the blind was the silhouette of the rat. He stood there in menacing profile. He raised his hand, pointing a bony claw at someone. Then his hand changed into a fist that he shook violently. Faint sounds of shouting reached Hermux's ears. But before Hermux could move, an enormous black limousine turned in from the main road and roared up Pickdorndle Lane, skidding to a stop in front of Ms Perflinger's house.

Darkened glass concealed the driver. He honked the horn briefly and raced the car's engine. Then the passenger door opened and a skinny white rat with blood-red eyes crawled out. He wore a torn black T-shirt that said LAB RAT in bold letters across the front. As he turned and walked towards the house the back of his T-shirt revealed a drawing of a rat with what looked like battery jump leads clamped on his ears. The rat's fur stood out in electric terror. His mouth was open in a scream. Scrawled below were the words

SHOCKING DEVELOPMENTS
Don't settle for inferior behaviour!
corporate rates

Chapter 22
BAD HOUSEKEEPING

The driver put the limo into gear and executed a clumsy and violent U-turn on the narrow street, lunging up over the kerbs, crushing a border of daffodils, and tearing several branches from Hermux's hiding-place in the rhododendron. He slammed the car into reverse and then screeched to a halt at Ms Perflinger's gate.

He rolled his window down, and Hermux could see him light a cigarette and toss the still-burning match on to the street.

'Animal!' thought Hermux.

Scratchy music from the car radio blasted through the air. It was *Caught in the Headlights* by RoadKill, one of Hermux's nephew's favourite bands. Hermux recognized it immediately.

Hermux instinctively put his fingers in his ears and ground his teeth. Then he saw that the upstairs light had gone out. Moments later the white rat emerged again on to the front porch accompanied by the grey rat and by Ms Perflinger! At least it was a mouse who was dressed like Ms Perflinger. The familiar red cap, the bright green feather, and the leather flight jacket. But all traces of Ms Perflinger's jauntiness were gone.

She moved slowly and awkwardly, with a rat supporting her at each elbow. They ushered her protectively to the limo. It seemed to Hermux that before she stepped into the car she glanced around her neighbour's yards hopefully, but it was hard to be sure. Her face was obscured by large sunglasses.

The grey rat snapped orders at the driver. The radio was turned off. The cigarette was tossed out of the window. The window was rolled up.

The limo sped off down the street, through the stop sign at the corner without even slowing, and fishtailed out into traffic.

Hermux rushed out on to the street, too late to do anything, but just in time to catch the number plate:

'Well, I bungled that rescue,' he said, discouraged. 'Now what am I supposed to do?'

He looked at Ms Perflinger's house. The gate hung open at the sidewalk. Then he made up his mind. He walked gingerly through the gate, closed it carefully behind him, and proceeded up the pavement and on to the front porch. He listened at the front door. There was nothing. He tried the handle. The door swung open easily. He stepped inside and locked the door behind him. He switched on the light, but even after a day full of surprises, he was not prepared for what met his eyes.

Linka's house was a terrible mess.

Hermux stepped from the small entrance hall into what

looked like the living-room. Or what might have been the living-room before it was buried beneath a thick layer of rubbish. There were pizza boxes and Chinese food containers and open soup cans and milk cartons and bread wrappers and whisky bottles and jam jars and cigarette packages and crisp packets. There were banana peels and apple cores and peanut shells and orange rinds and grape stems and biscuit crumbs and eggshells.

In the kitchen things were worse. The counter and the sink and the stove and the floor were coated with cake batter and ketchup and chocolate syrup and butter and spaghetti sauce and salt and pepper and sugar and hundreds and thousands and marshmallow fluff.

And there were dirty glasses and spoons and plates and saucers and cups and bowls and pans and knives. All scattered everywhere throughout the house. On the table. On the couch. On the television. On the rug. On the bookshelves. On the stairs. Next to the phone.

Hermux ran to the phone and dialled the police.

Chapter 23
EYEWITNESS REPORT

'Now slow down, Mr Tantamink,' the desk sergeant interrupted.

'Tantamoq. Tantamoq! It's -mock not -mink,' said Hermux into the phone.

'Naturally. Now, Mr Mock. Let's start at the beginning. You want to file a missing persons report for a Mrs Perflinger ...'

'Ms Perflinger.'

'Right. You say that Mrs Perflinger brought her watch in to be fixed. And then she forgot to pick it up.'

'No! I don't think she forgot at all. That's the point. I think she was prevented.'

'Right. Someone, probably a very sinister someone, prevented her from picking up her watch. And then you followed this someone to her home. And you saw a limousine drive up. And she got in it. And drove off.'

'She was wearing sunglasses!'

'Right. And she was wearing sunglasses at the time.'

'And her house is a mess! There are dirty dishes everywhere!'

'Right. Dirty dishes everywhere.'

'And I've got the licence number.'

'Let me just get all the details down. Caller has licence number. Now Mr Mock ...'

'Tantamoq!'

'Right. Mr Tantamoq. Just how well do you know Mrs Perflinger?'

'Well. I actually only met her the one time in my shop. But I've read about her, and I feel like I know her very well. She's a very special mouse.'

'Right. I'm sure she is a very special mouse. In fact I'm sure you're a very special mouse. But let's look at what we've got here. A lady forgets to pick up her watch. She's not a very good housekeeper. She rides around in a limousine. And she wears sunglasses. It's all very interesting, Mr Tantamoq. I just don't think it's necessarily a matter for the police.'

'But I'm sure she is in some sort of horrible trouble. She left with three very sneaky-looking rats.'

'Now careful there, Mr Tantamoq. I'm a rat myself. And proud of it. Let's not be calling any names.'

'I didn't mean just because they were rats. But they weren't very nice rats. They were the most unpleasant sort imaginable. Definitely not the kind that Ms Perflinger would be friends with. And they didn't act like friends at all ...' Hermux stopped. There was a creaking sound out on the porch. He looked to the front door. There was someone standing outside.

And then he saw the doorknob turn.

Chapter 24
PUSHING THE ENVELOPE

Hermux quietly hung up the phone. He looked around the room desperately for something to use as a weapon to defend himself. He picked up the potted plant on the table and crept towards the front door.

'Linka!' a feminine voice said. 'Are you home?'

Someone rapped briskly on the door. There was a pause. 'Listen, this was delivered to us by mistake. It's for you. Come over. We miss you!'

The brass mailbox in the door opened and a white envelope shot through the air and slid across the floor.

Hermux heard footsteps cross the porch and recede up the walk. He set the potted plant down and knelt to pick up the envelope. It was addressed to Linka Perflinger in a handsome flowing script. But it was the postmark and the return address that caught Hermux's attention.

It was from Dr Turfip Dandiffer, c/o The Hospital of the Kindly Friend, Pollonia, Teulabonari. It was postmarked two weeks ago in Teulabonari.

Hermux propped the letter up on the bookshelf where Ms

Perflinger would see it when she returned. He picked up the potted plant to return it to its place on the table. In doing so he brushed against the tight, glossy foliage, which released a pleasing spicy aroma somewhere between cinnamon and nutmeg.

'Hmmm,' said Hermux. 'That's very nice. I wonder what this is.'

He looked at the plant more closely. A white plastic stake was embedded in the dirt.

Water when thoroughly dry.

Hermux clawed delicately at the soil. It was as dry as sand.

'I'd say this is ready for water,' said Hermux. He went into the kitchen in search of a clean glass or cup. There was a cup in the sink lined with a thick scum of what looked like the ancient remains of tomato soup. Hermux scrubbed it out. And filled it with clean water which he carried to the plant in the living-room. He poured the water slowly over the soil. The moisture released another wave of the pleasant fragrance. This time with overtones of clove.

Hermux pinched off one of the small fleshy leaves. He broke it in two, sniffed it, and cautiously nibbled a bit from the edge.

'Hmmmm,' he repeated. 'It's got a very fresh taste to it.' He pocketed the remains of the leaf and turned the light out to leave.

At the front door he gave a last look around. In the semi-darkness of the living-room he could still clearly see the letter from Dr Dandiffer.

Hermux thought of Ms Perflinger. He remembered the awkward way she walked to the limousine. He remembered the gravelly voice of the grey rat. He thought of his conversation with the police sergeant. Then he crossed over to the bookshelves, took up Dandiffer's letter, and slipped it into his coat pocket.

'It may be a dangerous and confusing job. But it's mine to do,' he said grimly.

Then, making sure the front door was unlocked before he pulled it shut behind him, he slipped out into the night.

Chapter 25
OMINOUS DEVELOPMENTS

Hermux arrived home without incident. He fed Terfle. And then made his dinner of sardines on toast. He was too worried about Linka to be very hungry. While he ate he stared at Dandiffer's letter, which was propped against the salt and pepper shakers on the kitchen table. He had an odd feeling that the letter might hold a clue to Linka's disappearance.

After dinner he made tea. While the tea steeped, he turned the fire on again under the kettle. He got Dandiffer's letter from the table and held it over the kettle just as he had seen it done in movies.

'In for a penny, in for a pound,' he said grimly.

The steam worked. In moments the flap of the envelope began to loosen and curl as the glue softened. Hermux laid the envelope flat on the counter and, pulling very gently, he worked the flap open.

Then he slipped his paw inside and withdrew a single folded sheet of stationery.

He laid it on the tea-tray and then carried it all into his study.

'Well, Terfle,' he confided as he lowered himself into his reading chair. 'This is the beginning of a new career for me. Either as a detective or a jailbird. Only time will tell. If it turns out to be the latter I will be asking you for hints on decorating my cage.'

He poured his tea, adjusted his spectacles and opened the letter.

Dear Linka,

Things here have not been going well. I seem to have broken my leg rather badly. And will be here at the hospital recuperating for at least another week. The circumstances were rather unusual. As a precaution I have suspended the research expedition for now. I will fill you in on the details when I return.

I'm sorry to impose upon you again, but I must ask you another favour. I am sending you a package that contains the expedition log and some lab samples I prepared. Can you deliver it to Dr Jervutz at the Perriflot Institute? Just as you did the moon plant? It's terribly important that he gets it as soon as possible.

I can't explain everything now, but Jervutz suspects that someone at the Institute is intercepting his mail.

Sorry to be so mysterious. But the situation here has taken an ominous turn since your visit.

Sincerely,
Turfip Dandiffer, Ph.D.

'Well, that's odd,' thought Hermux. 'Things have taken an ominous turn here as well. And I'm no detective, but I can sense a connection. Tomorrow morning first thing I'll call Dr Jervutz and see what he'll tell me. Then I'll call Pup Schoonagliffen and find out if he can help me with that number plate.'

Hermux brushed his teeth and combed his whiskers and fur and then got ready to turn in. It had been a long, eventful day. He crawled into bed and turned off the light. But he couldn't sleep. He remembered the image of Ms Perflinger hidden behind her sunglasses glancing about the neighbourhood, looking for help. But was she looking for help? The police didn't think so.

He remembered Dandiffer's letter and its hints of danger in the jungle and intrigue at the Institute. He remembered the first day he had seen Ms Perflinger. He remembered her bold spirit. Her verve and her determination. And then he remembered that he hadn't written in his journal.

Tired as he was, he turned on the light, opened his journal, and uncapped his pen.

'What's to be thankful for today?' he wondered out loud.

As unnerving as it all was, he had to admit that he hadn't felt this stimulated in years. Not really since he'd prepared for his watchmaker's final examination. He set his pen to the paper and wrote.

> Thank you for surprises, for adventure. Thank you for nice mice like Blanda Nergup, for intrigue, for rascals like Nock Noddem, for sceptical policemen. Thank you for elevators and trams and newspapers. Thank you for friendly neighbours. For rules to follow and rules to break. And thank you in advance for a good night's sleep.

Chapter 26
UNEXPECTED OPTIMISM

The next morning as soon as it was light Hermux bounded out of bed. He raced to the bathroom, jumped into the shower, and scrubbed himself vigorously from head to toe. He whistled as he towelled himself dry. He hummed as he combed his fur straight. He smiled as he looked in the mirror. Even his whiskers seemed perkier than usual. He didn't stop to wax them.

'Goodness,' he thought. 'Ms Perflinger may be in mortal danger. Dr Dandiffer may be laid up with a broken leg. And odd things may be afoot at the Perriflot Institute. But despite it all I feel wonderful. In fact I feel like singing.'

And so he did. He sang to Terfle as he removed the cover from her cage. He sang while he made his toast. He sang while he cooked his porridge. And poured his orange juice. In fact it wasn't until he started eating that he stopped singing.

While he ate he jotted on a notepad.

Call Dr Jervutz
Call Pup S.
Inquire re: rat at Automated Laboratory Equipment

He tore off the sheet, folded it and put it in his pocket. Then he brushed his teeth and raced to the shop.

At 9.00 a.m. exactly he telephoned the Perriflot Institute.

'I'd like to speak to Dr Jervutz, please,' he told the switchboard operator. She put him through to Dr Jervutz's office.

But there was no answer.

He tried Pup at the *Daily Sentinel*.

'Mr Schoonagliffen is not due in until after eleven,' he was told. Hermux left his name and number and asked that Pup call.

That left Automated Laboratory Equipment. Hermux closed the shop and scurried off down Ferbosh Avenue. Flowerpots and window-boxes in front of the stores were bursting with daffodils and tulips.

'What a beautiful morning to be out adventuring!' he thought. The sun had burned through the clouds, and the city looked fresh and ready for spring. He turned on to Grandle Street, crossed over the tramlines, and walked straight to the Progressive Tower.

Inside the lobby was deserted, as it had been the day before. Hermux took the elevator up to the twenty-sixth floor. He strode purposefully down the hall past Abacus Instruction and Rentals, Accordion Repairs, Amusement Park Personnel, and Artificial Paws. He passed the Astral Projection Club and Attic Maintenance & Supplies.

He hesitated a moment in front of the door to Automated Laboratory Equipment. Then he grasped the doorknob firmly and stepped inside.

As the door closed silently behind him Hermux realized that he hadn't given any thought to what he was going to say.

'May I help you?' asked an earnest-looking squirrel in a spotless white lab coat. He was standing by a large packing crate, apparently checking off items on a shipping list.

For a moment Hermux's mind went completely blank. Then he saw the word Mennus scrawled on the end of the crate in grease pencil.

'I was just checking up on the order for Dr Mennus,' he sputtered.

'I'm just finishing it up. One ultra-sensitive chemical analyser and one high-speed concentrator. I've included the manuals and the set-up instructions for each of them. But tell Dr Mennus that I would still feel much better if we came out to the clinic and did the set-up ourselves.'

'Would you mind if I take a quick look at the packing list?' asked Hermux.

'Not at all,' said the squirrel, handing Hermux the clipboard. 'Everything is in order. I'll just get started sealing the crate. It should be out at the clinic early this afternoon.'

Hermux studied the list. The equipment was being shipped to:

Dr Hiril Mennus
Last Resort Health Spa & Research Clinic
Misty Valley Road
Pinchester

It was being billed to:

The Millennium Project
Tucka Mertslin Cosmetics.

Chapter 27
REVELATION

It was 11.00 by the time Hermux got back to the shop. He dialed the number for the Perriflot Institute.

Dr Jervutz was in.

'Dr Jervutz,' began Hermux. 'My name is Hermux Tantamoq, and I'm calling on behalf of Ms Linka Perflinger.'

'Ms Perflinger. Oh, yes. I remember her. She called several weeks ago and made an appointment with me. Rather mysterious type. She said she was delivering something important from Dr Dandiffer in Teulabonari. But she stood me up, and I haven't heard from her since. Does she wish to make another appointment?' he asked suspiciously.

'No. She is unavailable at the moment. It is I who would like to make an appointment. I have a letter from Dr Dandiffer which I would like to pass on to you.'

'Dandiffer! Good gosh, man! We lost contact with him two weeks ago. Radio went dead. No word at all! When can you come? I'll be free at the end of the day. Would five-thirty work?'

'Yes. I'll be there at five-thirty.'

'Fine. I'll tell security downstairs to expect you.'

'Dr Jervutz?' asked Hermux.

'Yes?'

'I wonder if I might ask just what Dr Dandiffer is doing in Teulabonari?'

'It's public knowledge, Tantamoq. Dr Dandiffer is an ethnobotanist. His speciality is the medicinal use of tropical plants.'

'What is he looking for?'

'He's working for me. I'm the director of the Perriflot Institute's Initiative on Ageing. Dr Dandiffer is looking for the Fountain of Youth.'

Chapter 28
YOUTHFUL PURSUITS

Hermux was relieved and perplexed by his conversation with Dr Jervutz. At least some pieces of the puzzle had fallen into place. Enough, thought Hermux, to prove that there actually was a puzzle.

The phone rang.

It was Pup.

'Tantamoq? Pup here. What's up?'

'Pup, I need to ask you a favour.'

'Anything at all, old man!'

'Can you check a number plate for me? I need to find someone.'

'Some little mousekins caught your eye, huh?' laughed Pup. 'And you want to track her down?'

'You might say that.'

'Okay, give it to me. It may take me a day or two to run it down. It depends on how busy my sources are.'

'The number is 2URHLTH,' Hermux said slowly and clearly.

'2URHLTH,' repeated Pup just as clearly. 'That should be

easy enough. I'll call you as soon as I have anything.' He hung up.

Hermux stared out of the front window on to the street, trying to put what he knew about Linka and Tucka and Dandiffer and Mennus together into a pattern that made sense.

'So it's all about youth,' he said, drawing a whisker out to its full length. Across the street a young chipmunk in a bright yellow playsuit was tearing the petals off the tulips in the flower-pot by Teasila Tentriff's door. Hermux opened the shop door and shouted at him. 'Hey, you, chipmunk! You stop that! You leave those flowers alone! You hear me?'

The chipmunk looked over at Hermux, tail twitching nervously. He still clutched a tulip in one paw. Half of the tulips were already picked clean, tall bare green stems waving in the spring breeze. The chipmunk moved off down the pavement, glancing back over his shoulder regularly to make sure Hermux wasn't chasing him.

But Hermux had already forgotten the chipmunk. There was something about the tulips that held his attention. Something he couldn't put his finger on. He clasped another whisker between his fingers and pulled it thoughtfully to its full length. 'That's odd,' he said. Not only didn't the tip of his whisker droop; it was positively curled into a corkscrew.

And that's when it hit him. It was the plant. The plant on Linka's table. 'It must be the same plant that Dandiffer sent back to Jervutz. Linka never delivered it. They must have been holding her prisoner in the house. That's why I'm feeling so good today. It was the plant that perked me up. I've got to get it before THEY do. Whoever THEY are!'

Once again Hermux closed the shop and hurried down the street. He waved cheerily at Teasila Tentriff, who had just arrived to find her tulips ruined. He tipped his hat at Earlin Bray, who was just coming down the courthouse steps. He scampered on to the tram platform and waited for a Number 3 to appear.

A Number 1 tram came first. Then a Number 4. And finally a Number 3. Hermux leapt on board and counted the stops impatiently until Pickdorndle Lane came into view. He pulled the cord to signal the driver and got off right in front of the grocery store.

'Gracious,' he said. 'I haven't eaten a thing since breakfast.' He checked his watch. It was nearly 2.00. 'No wonder I'm hungry. I'd better get a sandwich or I'll faint.'

The grocery store was cool and clean and had a wonderful smell of cheeses and nuts and corncakes and molasses. Hermux rang the bell at the glass deli counter and a heavy set bluejay came out of the back room wiping his wings on his apron.

'Can I get a cheese sandwich, please. With lettuce and mayo.'

'What kind of bread?' asked the bluejay.

'Nutty wheat.'

'Pickled grubs?'

'Yes. That sounds good.'

'Anything to drink?'

'I'll have a honey fizz.'

'Two dollars,' said the bluejay, handing Hermux a neatly folded paper bag. 'You need a napkin?'

'Please.'

Hermux walked slowly down Pickdorndle Lane towards Linka's. He tried to appear casual in case any of Linka's friendly neighbours were home. When he got to her gate he opened it quickly and went up the walk. He checked the street to see if anyone was watching, and then he let himself in the front door.

Everything seemed to be just as he left it. A terrible mess.

But in the living-room there was an unpleasant new surprise. The plant was gone. It had been there when he left last night. But now there was only a pale circle in the dust on the table where the pot had sat.

He clearly remembered returning the plant to the table. He looked in the kitchen. He looked by the telephone in the hall.

It was definitely gone.

There was a sharp rap at the front door, and Hermux nearly jumped out of his fur.

Chapter 29
HERMUX GOES POSTAL

'Package for Perflinger!' called a surprisingly familiar voice.

Hermux edged towards the front window and peeked through the curtain. There stood Lista Blenwipple with a parcel in her hands.

Hermux threw open the door.

'Lista, what a surprise to see you here!' he exclaimed with relief.

'Hermux, what a surprise to see you here!' answered Lista.

They stared at each other for a long uncomfortable moment. Then Hermux smiled.

'I'm house-sitting for a friend,' he told her, pulling the door closed behind him so Lista wouldn't see the mess in the living-room.

'Oh, of course! Your friend!' Lista smiled broadly. She would have something to talk about for the rest of the week. 'And where is she?'

'She's out of the country right now.' Hermux lowered his voice and spoke in a confidential tone. 'On a rather sensitive mission.'

'I won't breathe a word about it,' lied Lista without a moment's hesitation. She felt giddy with the excitement. Her heart was actually pounding. She thought about rearranging her route in the morning so she could start at Lanayda Prink's coffee shop. That would show Lanayda just who was in the know. But that wouldn't really do. The news would spread like wildfire from Lanayda's. No. She would have to hold Lanayda off until the very last. 'Sorry, Lanayda,' she thought. 'You'll just have to wait your turn. In this case the news takes precedence over the mail.'

'Is there something I need to sign?' asked Hermux.

'What?' Lista was startled out of her daydream.

'Do I need to sign something for Ms Perflinger's package?' He looked at her curiously. She seemed even more distracted than usual.

Lista handed Hermux the package and began to root around in her pockets. 'Mercy!' she said. 'It's here someplace. Oh, here it is. You can sign right there. Your name. And then below that write "for Linka Perflinger".'

Hermux took her pen and signed his name on the delivery slip.

'You realize that it's a little irregular letting you sign for her. But since I know you so well. And know how you and Ms Perflinger are ... well ... so close, it won't be a problem. But tell her next time she really should put in a vacation notice so I'll know she's off someplace.'

'Yes, you're absolutely right. I'll tell her just that. It won't happen again. Thank you for your trouble. I'll see you tomorrow morning then.'

Hermux took the package and stepped back inside.

Lista was positively beaming that day as she finished her deliveries on Pickdorndle Lane.

Chapter 30
IT ALL ADDS UP

'I hope that woman can keep a secret!' thought Hermux as he locked the door and watched Lista disappear down the sidewalk.

'I'm as hungry as a teenager. Excitement seems to build my appetite.'

He retrieved his lunch and looked around for a reasonably clean spot to sit and eat. There wasn't much to choose from. He finally settled on the foot of the stairs. He unwrapped his sandwich and bit into it greedily. The cheese was sharp and tangy with just a musky hint of mould. The bread was fresh and piled with fresh, crisp, and spicy watercress. He wrinkled his nose appreciatively and closed his eyes a moment while he chewed.

He uncapped the honey fizz and downed a healthy swig of it.

'Now I can think,' he said. And think he did. First, the plant was gone. The plant had something to do with Dandiffer's search for a youth formula. And judging from the way Hermux had been feeling all day, it seemed likely that the plant was one of the key ingredients. Second, Tucka and Dr Mennus were tied up in this somehow. Tucka seemed to have more problems than just packaging her youth formula. From the look of things, she didn't have a formula yet. Third, Dandiffer was mysteriously laid up in a hospital, cut off from communication, and he'd called off the expedition. Fourth, and most important as far as Hermux was concerned, Linka had been abducted. It was clear to him now that she had been held as a prisoner in her own house. And now she had been moved to somewhere more secure. Or ... Hermux didn't even want to consider the alternatives.

'Let's go back to the plant,' said Hermux out loud. It was easier for him to keep things straight if he actually said them. 'Obviously the rats who held her prisoner and then took her away knew nothing about the plant or they would have taken it. Either they forced her to reveal the existence of the plant or somehow they found out about the plant through other means. But I haven't mentioned it to anyone. Dr Jervutz might know about it. But surely he's on Dandiffer's side. Or is he?'

Hermux checked his watch. It was nearly time to leave for his appointment at the Perriflot Institute.

But before he left, he wanted to take a look upstairs. At the top of the stairs Hermux found a short hallway lined with framed photographs of Linka and her aeroplane. It was a small, silver, single-engine plane. Painted on the side of the engine was an insignia composed of a red heart with golden wings and beneath it the inscription: *Fly high! Be bold!* In one photo Linka waved from the cockpit. In another she stood laughing by the propeller. In another she knelt on the wing. In each one her bright face met Hermux eye-to-eye. He was

107

smitten all over again. He had to find her and make sure she was safe.

The front room was a bedroom, and that's where Hermux started his search. It was there that Hermux had seen the rat's shadow on the blind. It was obviously Linka's room, and it was immaculately clean. The bed was carefully made up with a white chenille bedspread.

'She is obviously not a poor housekeeper. I'm afraid she was the victim of unwanted guests.' He opened her wardrobe. Neat as a pin. He looked at her dressing-table. There was nothing out of place. He opened the drawer, half-expecting to find a note addressed to him asking for his help. He looked through the waste paper basket. But except for a quantity of tissues there was nothing. No crumpled distress call. No clue torn from a notepad.

He went back out into the hall and tried the other door. It was Linka's office. Or it had been before it had been turned upside down. The drawers of her desk had been dumped on the floor and ransacked. Every book on every shelf was thrown on to the floor. The pictures had been taken from the walls. The cushions on the chair had been cut open and the stuffing pulled out.

'Well, if there had been a clue there, it's gone now,' said Hermux. 'I'd think I'd better get out of here.'

He went downstairs and got Dandiffer's package. He gave a last look about the place and saw the remains of his lunch on the stairs.

'Tsk! Tsk! No reason for me to be rude,' he said. He gathered up the bottle, the bag and the sandwich wrapper and took them into the kitchen and dropped them into the bin.

Then he rummaged below the sink and found a shopping-bag. He put Dandiffer's package into it and prepared to leave. But before he did, he climbed the stairs again and stood before the photos of Ms Perflinger. He took down the one of her standing in front of the plane by the propeller. He went back down, slipped the photo into the shopping-bag next to the package, and set out for his appointment with Dr Jervutz.

Chapter 31
Too Late

From the window of the tram it looked like a street festival was in progress in front of the Perriflot Institute. The pavements were jammed with people. Whirling red and blue lights lit the crowd in carnival colours. But when Hermux got closer, he realized that the lights came from the tops of two police cars and an ambulance.

He threaded his way through the onlookers.

'What's happening?' he asked.

'There's been a murder!' said a worried-looking young mother. 'Someone's been killed at the Institute.'

'Who?' demanded Hermux.

'They haven't said! But someone important!'

The heavy bronze doors of the Institute swung open and the paramedics emerged with a stretcher. The crowd strained forward to see. Hermux stood on his very tippiest toes. He could make out the form of a stout body beneath the grey blanket that covered the stretcher.

'Tragic, isn't it?' said Pup Schoonagliffen, pushing his way past Hermux with a large press camera.

As the paramedics struggled to get the heavy stretcher up into the ambulance, the blanket caught on the door, revealing the body beneath it.

The flashbulb on Pup's camera exploded. The harsh light revealed a contorted figure in a torn and charred tweed suit. One arm was raised as if fending off a final blow. The twisted claws of the pale brown paw seemed to point accusingly in Hermux's direction.

'Who is it?' Hermux shouted to Pup.

Pup turned back to him, his large teeth flashing an eerie red in the ambulance light.

'Dr Jervutz,' he said, shaking his head sadly. 'Director of Research.'

Chapter 32
FEELING WOOZY

A wave of nausea swept over Hermux. Followed shortly by near panic. He clutched the shopping-bag close to him and eyed the crowd suspiciously. The murderer might still be there. He might even be watching Hermux at that very moment.

A car nosed its way through the crowd and stopped by the ambulance. The chauffeur opened the rear door for a tall, dignified mouse. Hermux recognized her as Ortolina Perriflot. Pup shoved his way forward and snapped her photo. In the glare of the flash it was obvious that she had been crying.

The policemen cleared a way through the crowd and escorted her up the steps and into the Institute. Hermux saw that Pup managed to slip in behind them.

After the ambulance left, the throng began to break up. Hermux stayed with a group that moved slowly back towards the tramline. It was a nervous, noisy bunch.

'Did you see the look of him?'

'He looked fried to me.'

'Might have been one of their experiments.'

'I've never liked that place!'

'Oh, nonsense! They do important work there. Medical work.'

'From the looks of him he could have used a doctor.'

'Too late for a doctor!'

Hermux listened carefully but didn't say a word. He avoided eye contact with anyone. And when the tram came, he waited until everyone else got on. Then he climbed aboard quickly and luckily found a place to sit. He slid the shopping-bag under his seat and clamped both his feet securely around it.

Nobody paid him any notice. Just another mouse among many making their way home from work.

Hermux did not go back to the shop. He went straight home. He made his way cautiously down the pathway of broken chunks of cement that led through the dark hallway to the lobby. He bent over the milk crate that had served as a communal mailbox since Tucka and Rink ripped out the wall of individual brass mailboxes. He sorted through piles and piles of other people's mail, finding a modest collection of bills for himself.

He got in the elevator and pressed 4. The door was just sliding closed when suddenly it stopped and then opened again.

A dark hooded figure filled the doorway and then began to glide noiselessly towards Hermux. Hermux backed further into the elevator. The frightening figure continued towards him. Hermux was ready to let out his most blood-curdling scream (he hoped).

But before he could make a sound, the figure spoke.

113

'Tantamoq! Great news about the bottle!' It was Tucka. She threw back her hood. Her face was completely covered with thick white make-up. Plastered, in fact. Her fur had vanished. On her head she wore a helmet that strongly resembled a skull.

Hermux gaped at her speechlessly.

'Oh, this!' Tucka laughed at him. 'It's my newest product. Foundation/Facial. You wear it all day. Peel it off at night. As good as a face-lift. But about the bottle! I saw the first prototype today. I must say Nergup surprised me. I didn't give her credit for that much imagination. We had some small problems when we cast the mould. But they'll get it pieced back together as good as new.'

'What do you mean, pieced back together?' asked Hermux indignantly.

'Exactly that. Once they've found all the pieces, they'll be putting the whole thing back together. We had no idea that old glass could be so fragile. You really should have warned us! But don't worry about that. I've already forgiven you.'

'You mean you broke the hourglass? The hourglass that my great-great-great-great-great-grandfather made? And that I loaned to you with the strictest understanding that it would be returned to me in perfect condition?'

'Great ghost of Cleopatra! You can't make an omelette without breaking an egg, Tantamoq. Sometimes I wonder how you get on in the world. Your precious hourglass will be returned to you in perfect condition.'

'Pieced together?'

'PERFECTLY pieced together! Are you deaf?' thundered Tucka.

114

'That isn't what we agreed upon at all,' argued Hermux. The elevator stopped. Tucka fumbled with the controls of her electric rollerblades.

'Really I would love to talk about this all evening. But I've got to rush to an important dinner,' she told him as she glided out of the elevator.

'Dinner with Dr Mennus?' retorted Hermux.

Tucka executed a hairpin U-turn in the hall and rolled imperiously to face Hermux.

'What do you know about that?' she demanded.

'Why, it's common knowledge, Tucka,' continued Hermux bravely. 'Mennus researching your youth formula. Running behind schedule. Budgets straining. Tempers flaring. Etc. Etc.'

'Whoever told you this is a completely vicious liar. There is not one iota of truth in any of it. And if you repeat a single word of it to anyone, I'll sue you for every pathetic cent you have!'

She stopped herself. 'Well, enough of that!' she said pleasantly. 'Lovely to see you as always!' She gave Hermux an evil little smile, threw her skates into reverse, and whizzed away down the hall waving a languid farewell with beautifully lacquered claws.

Chapter 33
ON THE PAPER TRAIL

Hermux was too jangled to warm up his acorn casserole in the oven. He stood with it next to the sink and ate a couple of cold spoonfuls right out of the pan. Then he put it back in the refrigerator and opened a box of crackers. He wandered back to his study, munching slowly, pondering the unsettling events of the day, and studying the package from Dr Dandiffer that sat expectantly at the centre of his desk.

Terfle ruffled her wings noisily in her cage.

'Oh, gosh, Terfle!' said Hermux. 'I completely forgot you. And look! Your cage is a mess. I'm sorry. I'll get right on it.'

Hermux opened the door to Terfle's cage and extended his paw to Terfle's perch. He nudged her front legs, and she climbed slowly on to his wrist.

'You're putting on weight, Terfle. Goodness, I've got to get you outside for some exercise. I'll call Mirrin tomorrow and see if I can bring you over for an afternoon in her garden.'

Terfle marched her way up Hermux's arm and settled on his shoulder, nuzzling her hard head against his neck. Hermux slid the bottom tray out of the cage and carried it over to the wastebasket. He dumped it carefully. Then he peeled up the newspaper, crumpled it and dropped it in the trash.

Then he laid the cage bottom on a sheet of newspaper, traced it with pencil, and used his silver heron scissors to cut out the shape. He fitted the new liner into the tray and replaced it in the cage. He carried Terfle's water bowl and food bowl into the kitchen and washed them carefully, filled up the water bowl with fresh water, and sprinkled an extra big handful of dried aphids into the food bowl.

'Tomorrow we'll start you on a little diet,' he told her. 'But you'll need your energy tonight. I've got a lot to tell you.'

He took her gently from his shoulder and placed her back on her perch. She jumped down immediately and ran to eat.

'Well, then,' Hermux announced as he returned to the kitchen. 'I think a pot of tea would be just the thing to calm my nerves and clear my head.' When the tea was ready, he added a box of chocolate shortbread biscuits to the tray and carried it back to the study.

'Let me just brief you on my day so far,' he told Terfle. And he recounted all the details from the time he first tried calling Dr Jervutz, to his visit to Automated Laboratory Equipment, to arriving at Linka's house, to Dr Jervutz's murder, to the nerve-racking encounter with Tucka in the elevator.

'I was going to give Dandiffer's journals to Dr Jervutz so he could put everything right. But now he's dead. And my great-great-great-great-great-grandfather's hourglass is smashed. And to top everything off I blew up at Tucka just now so now she knows that I know about her and Mennus. So if she's the murderer, I suppose I'm as good as dead already. And if Mennus is the murderer, I probably won't be as good as dead until tomorrow. Which gives me this evening to get this figured out.'

He took a sip of tea and walked over to his desk.

'Well, I've got the journal,' he said, setting down his tea. 'I may as well find out if there's anything in it.'

He snipped the twine with his scissors. He removed the brown paper wrapper, cut out the Teulabonari stamps and set them aside for his nephew. Then he opened the carton. Inside were a green ledger volume and a cigar box sealed with tape.

Chapter 34
DR DANDIFFER'S JOURNAL

Day one. Pollonia–Teulabonari

Docked late last night. Up early this morning to oversee unloading. Some damage evident from the last storm. Won't know extent until tomorrow when we uncrate and transfer to the upriver boat. Halfway through unloading, the police arrived and shut us down. More problems with papers and permits. One of the other passengers was very helpful. Speaks Teula better than me. Gaspell Bermillonk–a medical student who's down to work for a term in a village clinic. And quite the diplomat. Police departed amicably. We finished unloading by sunset. I've invited Gaspell to join me for dinner. Will sound him out about possibility of joining the expedition. With his medical experience he would be very handy to have around.

Day two–River Nogonda

Great luck last night. Bermillonk's clinic was closed without notice for one month. He'll join us until it re-opens. Spent the morning with him in my cabin reviewing my notes and maps from the first expedition. Bright fellow. He gets along well with the others. Except for Glower, who I think is a little jealous. But he'll get over it.

Day three—Ilinoris Junction

By noon we had entered the jungle. Now the river is like a tunnel cut through a mountain of emeralds. Heavy rains in the afternoon as we docked. Followed by much excitement at dinner. Glower found a python in his cabin. Apparently crawled up out of the cargo hold. It took three of the crew to wrestle it overboard. Glower got a bad squeeze. His ribs are bruised, and he's shaken up. Gaspell has volunteered to oversee hiring the porters tomorrow while I see to the provisioning.

Day four—Lower mountain camp

Luckily we're high enough to take an edge off the heat. Hope that helps revive Glower. His stomach is bothering him. We had to carry him halfway up the mountain. Lucky I've got Gaspell now to help out. Tomorrow we've got to unpack and set up the lab equipment and the radio.

Day five—Lower mountain camp

Glower's having a rough time of it. Exhaustion. Fever. Chills. Poor guy. Hope this isn't Tugg Fever.

Lab and radio set up. Sent a message to Jervutz confirming our arrival.

I left a package of gifts for the Nerrans this afternoon at their meeting tree. (1 box matches. 1 magnifying glass. 1 package of sewing needles. 1 spool of waxed linen thread. 1 bottle of aspirin.)

Day six–Lower mountain camp

I hiked out to the meeting tree after breakfast. The Nerrans had left a woven bark basket of gifts for me. (1 miniature orchid. 1 bundle of dried and shredded bark. A necklace of iridescent beetle wings. A nutshell filled with a dark aromatic paste. And a dried banana leaf rolled up into a scroll. On the banana leaf a drawing: Two figures seated beneath the meeting tree. The sun directly overhead.)

It was a message from Tinán, the shaman. He would meet me at the tree tomorrow at noon.

Off to a great beginning!

Back at camp. Glower's taken a turn for the worse. He's delirious now. Told me that Gaspell sneaks into his tent when I'm gone and gives him injections.

Gaspell is pretty sure it's Tugg Fever. Penicillin would stop it. But I checked the medical kit, and there isn't any. Possibly it was pilfered when we repacked at the Junction. We're also missing mosquito nets, and we're short on coffee, sugar, flour, kerosene, and batteries for the radio. I radioed Jervutz at the Institute and requested emergency supplies. Hope they get here in time. For Glower's sake.

For now all we can do is give him liquids and try to keep him cool while he rides it out.

Day seven–Lower mountain camp

Met with Tinán. I wish these people could get to the point. Almost two hours of greetings, more exchanges of gifts, ritual tea drinking, and chewing nardle nuts. And finally to business. He will take me up on to the mountain (price: two working flashlights). He will show me where the moon plant grows and

121

how to harvest it (price: one camp stove). If the signs are auspicious, he will permit me to watch the preparation of the earth crystals (price: two tents). And if the tribe consents, I can observe the Renewal Ritual at the Spring Equinox (price: one radio). If things go as planned, we should be returning to the Junction in two weeks with the youth formula. And with a lot less equipment for the porters to carry.

Message from Jervutz. Emergency supplies en route. Should be here tomorrow. Hope Glower can hold on. He looks bad.

On the way back from Glower's tent I thought I heard voices in the lab tent. The flap was closed but there was a light on inside. It gave me a start. It was just Gaspell. He said he was anxious to get started analysing the shredded bark and the aromatic paste from the Nerrans.

'I thought I heard voices,' I told him.

'Oh, I apologize. I have a habit of thinking out loud when I'm working.'

Lucky I stopped in, though. I noticed that the radio had been left on. With only one spare battery left, we've got to be more careful.

Day eight–Lower mountain camp

We found a level clearing nearby to use as a landing strip. Spent the day clearing rocks. Picked up a radio signal late in the afternoon. Landed without any hitches. Then a big surprise! The pilot is a woman. Linka Perflinger. Professional adventuress. I must say I'm impressed. Trained as a nurse too. She asked to see Glower immediately. She gave him the penicillin herself. And then volunteered to sit with him. Tonight is the full moon. I go with Tinán for the moon plant harvest. Gaspell got very argumentative about coming with us. But I know Tinán too well. Our bargain was that I would come. I didn't specify an assistant. Gaspell finally gave in. But I'm a little uncomfortable. I know gophers can really hold a grudge.

Day nine–Lower mountain camp
I'm exhausted this morning but the smell of fresh coffee roused me out of my tent. Miss Perflinger and Gaspell were already at breakfast. She informed me immediately that Glower's fever was down, and that he had slept through the night.
They were both extremely curious to hear about my night with Tinán. I told them everything. The climb up the mountain with Tinán and his niece guiding me blindfolded in the dark. The change in feeling as we left the rainforest and entered the cloud forest. Having my blindfold finally removed at the top of the mountain. And the astonishing experience of finding myself above the clouds, beneath a moon that seemed so big I could reach out and touch it. But there was no time for admiring the scenery. Tinán and his niece set to work immediately, gathering the new leaves on the moon plants. They showed me how to recognize the plants by the dull glow that the mature leaves gave off in the moonlight.
And then after hours of gathering, the return trip. Blindfolded again.
What I didn't tell Miss Perflinger or Gaspell was that for the price of an additional camp stove and five gallons of kerosene, Tinán allowed me to dig up a healthy specimen of moon plant. And that it was safely wrapped in a burlap bag in my tent. I'm not sure why I hesitated to mention it. I showed them the bag

of leaves I had harvested. Gaspell was hot to get started on the analysis and disappeared with them to the lab tent.

Miss Perflinger was anxious to get started on her return flight before it got any later. I asked her if she would take a package to Dr Jervutz at the Institute. She consented readily. And while she checked on Glower again, I returned to my tent to pack the moon plant for the long trip.

Then she and I walked out to the landing strip together. She told me that she had followed my first expedition with great interest and asked if it was really true that the Nerrans did not age.

I explained how I had discovered the Nerrans by following the legends of the 'ageless ones' which told how a tribe of chinchillas had vanished in the cloud forest generations ago. How they were seldom seen by outsiders. But in the rare reports of encounters with the tribe, it was noted that they did not seem to age past maturity. Once they were grown to adulthood, they remained unchanged. And the only deaths that were reported were apparently due to accidents and the occasional act of violence.

I told her how, after three trips to the area, I had finally succeeded in meeting Tinán last year and how, after months of enigmatic encounters at the meeting tree, I had managed to establish a relationship with him and persuaded him to share some of his knowledge of the ageing process with me. That's why I was here now. For the Renewal Ritual which takes place at the Equinox.

I explained that the Perriflot Institute was now funding my efforts, and that I was working under the direction of Dr Jervutz.

After a week of Glower and Gaspell it was a pleasure to talk to someone as bright and inquisitive as Miss Perflinger.

I have to admit that I was sorry when we reached her plane. She stowed my parcel. And then shook hands with me.

'I'm honoured to have been able to assist such a noble and fascinating effort,' she told me. And I believe she meant it.

'Oh, may I ask a favour of you?' she said.

'Naturally,' I told her.

'Would you take a picture of me with the plane? It's a bit of a tradition with me. I like to have a picture of each of my adventures.'

She gave me her camera. And I took her picture. Standing there bravely in front of her plane. With the mist rising from the jungle.

Then she climbed aboard, taxied down our rough and tumble runway, and took off into the immense blue sky, tipping her wings goodbye.

Chapter 35
INTERMISSION

'I have a bad feeling about this Gaspell Bermillonk,' Hermux told Terfle, closing the journal and rubbing his eyes. 'And I'm not saying that because he's a gopher. There was a gopher family in Tucka's apartment for years before she bought them out. And they were perfectly nice. Although I can't say I miss the smell of boiled lily tubers.'

He took another sip of tea, but it was cold. He shook the box of biscuits, but he'd eaten every one.

'A good mystery certainly stimulates my appetite,' he announced. He glanced at Terfle's food bowl. 'Yours too from the look of things!'

Terfle fixed her beady black eyes on him hopefully.

'All right,' Hermux conceded. 'A little extra snack just once won't hurt either one of us.'

Five minutes later Hermux returned from the kitchen with a loaded tray. A bottle of ginger beer, bread and butter, and a little pot of extra-stinky cheese. Plus a surprise for Terfle–a package of pear twigs covered with mussel scale. Hermux tore open the foil and fastened a pear twig to a clip on one of the bars of Terfle's cage. She scooted down her perch and began to devour the crunchy scale like popcorn.

Hermux spread some extra-stinky cheese on a piece of bread and watched Terfle contentedly.

'I just don't like the way Gaspell showed up so conveniently out of nowhere,' Hermux went on with his mouth full. 'Doesn't sound like Glower trusted him. But then Glower is put out of commission right away and Gaspell takes over his job. Supplies disappear, and Dandiffer still doesn't seem to notice any pattern in what's happening. But maybe it's a lot easier to see a pattern from a distance. At least he's kept his mouth shut so far about the moon plant.'

Terfle continued grazing hungrily along the pear twig without looking up.

Hermux opened Dandiffer's journal and went back to reading.

Chapter 36
FROM BAD TO WORSE

Day ten–Lower mountain camp

Glower much improved. Tomorrow I move up on to the mountain to establish camp near the Nerran village. I will observe preparations for the Ritual of Renewal while Glower and Gaspell complete our plant collections here. Things are getting back on track.

I spoke with Jervutz via radio tonight. He sounded very odd. He says that my field notes from last year's expedition are missing from the lab. Also he says he is being watched. And he thinks the lock on his desk has been tampered with. A little paranoid, I think. I wonder if the pressure of running the Institute is starting to get to him. We got cut off by interference. I'll try to reach him again tomorrow night.

Day eleven–Lower mountain camp

Bad luck is back. The batteries for the radio have disappeared. We might be able to replace them at the Junction, but it would cost us days of work. Gaspell thinks Tinán stole the batteries. That's hard for me to believe. The radio and the batteries will be his in two weeks. What's the hurry? But who else is there? The porters have no use for batteries. They have no particular value. And they're too heavy to lug very far in this jungle.

Day twelve–Upper mountain camp
Unpleasant scene with Gaspell this morning. He got himself worked up again about coming with me and the Nerrans. I explained again that it's out of the question, and that it is crucial for us to complete the botanical survey. He resents working under Glower. He got very agitated and for a brief moment I actually thought he was going to strike me. Astonishing. Then he recovered himself and became quite cheerful again. The isolation is getting to him. The jungle affects everyone differently. Glower is a good steady influence. I think he'll shape him up.

Arrived near the Nerran village at dusk and set up camp without incident. Tinán and his niece brought me a basket of small reddish fruits, which they showed me how to peel and eat. The skin is tough and bitter. The flesh is nearly transparent. Very sweet and sticky. Like a candied lemon.

Day thirteen–Upper mountain camp
Tinán appeared early and escorted me into the village. I was immediately struck by the absence of any elders. There was not a single old person anywhere. Once they reach maturity the Nerrans simply seem to cease ageing. They are a handsome and vigorous-looking people. My appearance provoked much laughter. Particularly my eyeglasses. They asked why my fur is dull. And why my teeth are yellow. And whether all my

people are old and decrepit like me. They call me Grandfather Time and Ancient One from Faraway.

Tinán showed me the medicine hut where the moon plant leaves are pounded into pulp, cooked very slowly in great copper pots, cooled, and then strained through a fine gauze woven of spider silk.

In the afternoon the youngsters assembled in front of the medicine hut. They were dressed in barkcloth vests fringed and embroidered with cowrie shells. Tinán led them out of the village in single file along a faint trail that ran through the jungle to the edge of a deep gorge. We followed the gorge for some distance until we reached an enormous stand of bamboo. Tinán and one of the older boys cut several lengths of bamboo. And carrying those, we descended a narrow staircase cut into the stone wall of the gorge until we reached the entrance of a cave. Tinán lit a torch and we followed him inside. The walls of the cave were limestone. Across the ceiling ran a narrow vein of amber crystals. At a signal from Tinán the children cut and lashed the bamboo together to form two long ladders which they erected and held in place while the two smallest children scaled them and began to scrape the crystals into small baskets.

'Each year we harvest the crystals. Each year they return again,' Tinán explained to me.

When the baskets were full the children descended. The older boys used their machetes to break up the ladders. The children gathered up all the bamboo scraps, carried them from the cave, and dumped them unceremoniously into the gorge. There was no trace of our visit to the cave. The small children led the way back to the village proudly carrying their crystal-laden baskets.

I later managed to bargain with Tinán for a small vial of the crystals, which I believe to be some sort of sulphur compound (price: my army knife).

Tomorrow at dawn the Ritual of Renewal begins.

Chapter 37
A WELCOME ALLY

The phone rang, startling Hermux out of Dandiffer's journal. Hermux lifted the receiver.

'Good evening, Hermux Tantamoq speaking.'

'Tantamoq?'

'Yes.'

'Schoonagliffen here. I'm glad I caught you! Interesting news on your number plate. Whoever your friend is, she's dating a very tough customer.'

'What you do mean?' asked Hermux.

'Number plate 2URHLTH is registered to none other than the rather sinister Dr Hiril Mennus.'

'Oh, no!' Hermux's fears were confirmed. 'Who is he?'

'I'm not entirely sure. I've only heard rumours.'

'Well, what is he doing here?'

'I don't know much. Odd fellow. He's runs a beauty spa and clinic west of the city. We get the occasional strange report. Nothing concrete. Listen, you sound worried. I tell you what. Why don't I go down to the morgue and see what I can dig up?'

'The morgue?' squeaked Hermux. 'Why the morgue?'

'The newspaper morgue. Not the county morgue. Old articles. Not corpses. I'll see what we've got in print on Mennus. Then why don't I come over to your place in the morning and show you what I've come up with?'

'Well, I'd appreciate that. Thank you. That's very kind of you. You're sure you don't mind?'

'Nonsense. I smell the makings of a story here. Maybe you can fill me in on your little friend. Whoever she is. Whatever's going on.'

'Well.' Hermux hesitated. 'Maybe you're right. Maybe I should tell you everything. Maybe you can help me figure out what to do next?'

'That's the spirit, old mouse! See you tomorrow.'

Hermux put down the phone and turned again to Dandiffer's journal.

Chapter 38
DR DANDIFFER'S JOURNAL
CONCLUDES

Day fourteen–Upper mountain camp

I woke to wild sounds of children shrieking and singing outside my tent. When I stepped outside they surrounded me, tickling and pinching me until I lay on the ground laughing so uncontrollably that I was afraid I would wet my pants. Fortunately Tinán appeared and explained that I must appease them by giving them something. I offered them a chocolate bar, which they refused indignantly. I finally understood that I was to give them something that was mine. In desperation I gave them my house slippers. Which I foolishly hoped would be returned to me. Tinán indicated that they should be satisfied and they departed. I dressed hurriedly and followed them to the village.

The scene there was chaotic. Swarms of children dragging clothes and furniture from the houses and piling them in the centre. I flinched as I saw my lovely comfortable old slippers thrown carelessly on to the heap. And then I smelled the smoke. Tinán emerged from the medicine hut with a lighted torch that he handed to one of the older girls. She circled the mound, setting fire to the discarded belongings as the adults emerged from their homes clad in fresh white garments and singing a lilting chorus. The children greeted their appearance with much hilarity, pelting them with handfuls of grain and hurling insults about their aged appearances and declining powers.

The grown-ups formed a ring around the bonfire that was blazing very pleasantly in the still chill morning.

Tinán appeared again, carrying before him a painted gourd. His niece accompanied him. She bore a small but ornate copper cup. Raising the gourd to the sun, Tinán made a short speech of thanks for the beginning of another year. Then he poured out a small amount of dark liquid into the copper cup. His niece presented the cup to the nearest villager. He raised the cup first to the sun and then to the other villagers as a toast, then he drank its contents. But he did not swallow it. He swished the liquid back and forth in his mouth like a wine taster–three times. And then with a dramatic gesture he spat it into the fire and wiped his mouth carefully on his sleeve.

Each of the adult villagers followed suit. And Tinán last of all–spitting grandly into the remains of the bonfire which by then had burned down to coals. At that, the children appeared with baking stones that they set carefully among the glowing coals. The mothers of the village returned to their houses and came back with bowls of dough which they formed into flattened doll shapes, decorated with dried fruits and nuts and set to cook on the hot stones. The smells of baking sweet cakes filled the air along with a general air of merriment.

The hot cakes were soon being devoured by hungry children and adults alike, and I was welcomed to join the festivities.

135

After breakfast the atmosphere of high jinks continued to build, and the rest of the morning was spent in spirited play which the adults entered into wholeheartedly. It culminated in an enormous village-wide game of hide-and-seek that lasted for nearly two hours.

Once it was over we gathered again in the centre of the village for lunch and then everyone retired, exhausted, to their homes for an extended siesta.

Day fourteen continued–Lower mountain camp

When I awoke I began to pack and break camp. Tinán arrived in the late afternoon looking remarkably refreshed. I noticed immediately that the small scar over his lip had faded. He came to collect my army knife, but he brought with him a special and unexpected gift–the gourd and the remains of the renewal serum from the ritual. I was quite shocked because he had made it clear earlier that I would have to bargain for it. He made me understand that what he was doing was a very serious business. That I must be very careful with it. That I must not drink it. And that it must not fall into the wrong hands.

I gave him my solemn promise on each count.

I was so flushed with my success that I fairly flew down the mountain. The camp was deserted when I arrived and I assumed that Gaspell had taken the entire crew with him to collect botanical samples. I opened up the lab tent and set to work at once analysing the renewal serum.

By the time I had determined the formula it was long past dark. As I copied it out carefully from my notes I heard a commotion outside. Gaspell lunged through the doorway of the tent and collapsed into a chair.

136

'I've got it!' I shouted at him. 'I've got the formula!'

Gaspell only stared back.

'Goodness!' I said. 'What's happened to you?'

'We were attacked!' he said. 'The porters! Glower's dead!'

His hands and face were covered with scratches and cuts. I cleaned and bandaged them. Got some food in him and got him to tell me the whole story from the beginning. It was garbled and hard to follow. He had awakened that morning to Glower's screams and run to his assistance. But arrived too late to save him. The porters had attacked him next, but he had managed to drive them away. He had buried Glower's body and then pursued the porters into the jungle where he'd finally lost them.

Telling the story took the last of his strength, and once he'd finished he fell into an exhausted sleep.

I returned to my tent in astonishment. I lay awake trying to fit the pieces of this mystifying puzzle together. Poor Glower! I never properly thanked him for his years of hard work and devotion. How will I ever break the news to his family?

Day fifteen–Illinoris Junction

It must have been 2.00 in the morning when I woke up. I thought I heard voices. And, listening more carefully, I realized it was Gaspell.

I got up and peered cautiously outside. There was a faint light coming from inside the lab tent. I got my shoes on, strapped on my revolver and crept silently towards the light. It was definitely Gaspell's voice. But who was he talking to?

I could see his shadow against the wall of the tent. He was sitting at the radio with the headsets on.

137

'Stop worrying, Mennus,' he said excitedly. 'It's all gone according to plan. Glower's out of the way. Dandiffer's cracked the formula, and I'll take care of him tomorrow. I've prepared a little surprise for him on the trail back down.'

I finally understood the bad luck we'd had since we left the dock at Pollonia. It had been Gaspell all along. He'd murdered Glower. He'd hidden the radio batteries to cut off our communications.

'Of course I've got the formula,' he went on in an irritated voice. 'The half-wit wrote it out and left it here in the lab. I can give it to you right now. Let me move the light so I can read it.'

I only had a moment to respond. I slipped my hand beneath the tent canvas and felt around on the floor for the battery pack.

'Okay,' said Gaspell. 'Are you ready?'

My fingers met the thick rubbery battery cable. I grabbed it and jerked with all my might.

The radio crashed to the floor. Gaspell let out a yelp of fear. I ran to the door of the tent and aimed my pistol at him.

'Get your hands up and get away from the radio, you doublecrossing gopher!'

He bared his teeth at me, but he backed away slowly.

'It was you all along, wasn't it?' I accused him. 'You'll pay for this. I'll see that you hang for Glower's death.'

'You'll see nothing, you old fool,' he hissed and with a deft kick and a shove he heaved the worktable and the radio towards me. I tried to scramble out of the way, but I tripped. I lost my grip on the pistol. The table crashed on to my leg. I felt a horrible blinding pain. And the lantern broke. In moments the tent was engulfed in flames.

'And so the career of the illustrious Dr Turfip Dandiffer ends tragically in the jungle of Teulabonari,' Gaspell gloated. 'It's a pity that your research won't be published. At least under your name.'

I could see him in the eerie light of the fire. He had the formula in one hand. And the test tube with the last of the serum in the other.

'Well, I've got to be going,' he announced sarcastically. 'I'll just have a little drink for the road.'

'Don't drink it, Gaspell,' I gasped.

'Why let it go to waste?' he asked. 'Why should I get old and stupid like you?'

As he raised the test tube to his lips, I managed to get my hand back on my pistol. I got off a single clean shot. The test tube shattered, spraying the serum all over his hands and face.

'Put the formula down,' I told him.

'Naturally, Doctor,' he said, licking his lips and eyeing me shiftily. Then he licked his fingers. 'Most delicious,' he chuckled.

'Spit that out! You impudent rascal!'

'Too late!' said Gaspell triumphantly. 'I already swallowed it. And you can shoot me if you want. But then who's going to get you out of this tent before you barbecue?'

Then he let out a squeak. And then a squeal. And then a quiver. And he began to shrink before my very eyes.

Meanwhile I struggled to free myself from the table. My left leg was badly broken and useless. I was in dreadful shape. I managed to crawl around the table and found to my astonishment the khaki jacket and shorts that Gaspell had been wearing–empty on the floor. He had vanished.

Then I saw a small rustling among the clothes. And lifting up

Gaspell's jacket, I found a tiny gopher that looked no more than a few hours old. I remembered Tinán's warning.

The serum was too powerful to be swallowed.

I grabbed the formula from the floor and stuffed it in my pocket. Cradling Gaspell in one arm, I half crawled and half squirmed out of the tent, just managing to clear the doorway before it collapsed in a flaming heap.

Hours later someone shook me roughly. It was Tinán. They had seen the fire from the mountain and come down to investigate. He bound and set my leg. He and the villagers helped me search the camp. We found Glower's grave at the edge of the landing strip and set a stone to mark it. The radio was destroyed in the fire. Much to Tinán's undisguised displeasure. I assured him that I would return on my next expedition and deliver a new working radio. The vial of sulphur crystals from the cave survived, but all that remained of the moon plant leaves was a fragile trace of ash.

The Nerrans helped me back down, spiriting me into town and disappearing without being seen by a single soul. There is a downriver boat this afternoon.

Ironically it looks like Gaspell will get his wish for eternal youth after all. Tinán's niece adopted him and took him back to the village, where he will be raised as a Nerran. I wonder as he grows up if he will have any recollection of how he got there?

Day sixteen–Hospital of the Kindly Friend, Pollonia, Teulabonari

The doctors removed Tinán's splint and binding and examined my leg carefully. They are amazed that I have been able to move, much less trek through the jungle. But it has taken its toll. My leg is badly swollen. I'm running a fever. My orders are total bed rest for at least two weeks.

Jervutz,

I am sending this off by air post and hope you receive it quickly. The formula is enclosed. Along with the sulphur crystals, which act as some sort of catalyst for the moon plant. We are definitely on the verge of a very important discovery. But it's not without danger. Be careful! You were right about being spied upon. Now it's gone beyond spying. Whoever they are, they apparently intend to stop at nothing to get the formula. The only clue I have is the name Mennus. Does it mean anything to you?

To avoid the chance of its being intercepted at the Institute, I am sending this via Ms Perflinger, who brought you the moon plant. Please show her every courtesy.

Chapter 39
SECURITY MEASURES

Hermux finished reading and looked up.

'Looks like I've put my foot in it now,' he confided to Terfle. 'I've gotten us mixed up with spies, thieves and killers. I wonder how long it will take them to fit me into the picture?'

A folded sheet of yellow paper was stuck between the last pages of Dandiffer's journal. Hermux unfolded it and examined the curious symbols that covered it.

'This must be the chemical formula for the Nerrans' youth serum. And there are notes here for preparing the moon plant leaves. I don't feel very comfortable having this around. Three people have already died for it. Or rather two people, if you don't count Gaspell, who didn't exactly die, but had to start all over. We'd better see what's in the cigar box.'

He used his letter opener to cut the tape and opened the box. Nestled in a bed of crumpled newspapers was a small glass vial of yellow and amber crystals. Hermux held it up to the light and shook it lightly. It was the consistency of lumpy sand.

The phone jangled suddenly, and Hermux nearly dropped the vial.

'It's very late to be calling,' thought Hermux. He lifted the receiver. 'Hermux Tantamoq speaking,' he answered cautiously.

There was dead silence on the line.

'Hello?' said Hermux. 'Hello?'

He listened carefully. But there was no one there. Hermux hung up the phone.

'Not a good sign, Terfle. The game is afoot. And I'm afraid we're playing whether we want to or not. I need to think this through carefully before ...'

An anguished cry from the hallway interrupted him.

He motioned to Terfle to be quiet and then crept stealthily to the front door. He fixed his eye to the peephole and peered down the hall. Someone, a shimmering figure of light, appeared to be fighting for his or her life in front of the elevator. There was another cry—this time victorious—and the figure spun free of the elevator and crashed into the wall opposite, showering the floor with sparkling bits of broken glass. It was Tucka. And she was furious.

Her mirrored cape was torn, and one of the antlers of her headdress had broken. She snapped it off and shook it in Hermux's direction. 'Incompetent moron!' she shouted. 'This elevator mechanism is completely inadequate for evening wear! I'm deducting the cost of this from my monthly maintenance!'

Kicking up a haze of mirrored dust, she stormed down the hall to her apartment.

'Thank goodness!' thought Hermux. 'It's only Tucka.' And then he caught himself. Tucka was probably mixed up in all this. She might even be the mastermind behind it.

He walked back to his study and stood for a moment lost in thought. Then he clapped his hands and sprang into action.

'The first order of business is this formula. It can't fall into the wrong hands,' he told Terfle. 'I could take it to the shop and put it in the safe. But I think that would be the first place they would look.'

He looked to Terfle for agreement. She watched him without moving.

'Or I could hide it in one of my books,' he said, indicating the crowded bookshelves. 'I could put it in the refrigerator. Or under my bed. Or in the dirty clothes.'

Terfle seemed unimpressed. He stared at her. 'Or ...' he said with a smile. 'I could let you watch over it.'

He slid the tray bottom out of Terfle's cage. He lifted up the newspaper liner, refolded the formula and slipped it beneath the newspaper.

'There,' he said proudly. 'Now you're Terfle the Watchbird. Be vigilant! Now for the journal. What's the last place anyone would look?'

He paced about the study. He inspected the kitchen. He examined the bathroom and poked about his bedroom. And then he stopped.

'Now that's an interesting idea,' he thought. He went back to the study and got the journal. Then he walked to the front door and peered through the peephole. The hall was deserted. He looked at his watch. It was past 11.00.

Hermux opened the door silently and tiptoed down the hall, avoiding tiny, crunchy shards of broken mirror. He stopped at the stairs and listened. Then slowly, one step at a time, he descended. The building was silent. Almost too silent. And Hermux was careful not to make a sound.

When he reached the lobby he remained in the shadows while he surveyed the scene. It was empty. He studied the front door for movement. When he was satisfied that he wasn't being observed, he crossed the lobby quickly, ducked under the crime scene tape and stepped over the brass plaque set into the floor. Hermux snorted as he read it.

STREET LIFE
by
RINK FIRSHEEN

Made possible by a generous grant from
TUCKA MERTSLIN COSMETICS

'I won't hold my breath until we get the cheque,' he thought.

He knelt beside the chalk outline of Tucka's body and opened the discarded handbag. He placed Dandiffer's journal inside it. Then he snapped it securely shut and replaced it exactly where it had lain.

Then with a look of grim satisfaction, he ascended the stairs as quietly as he had come and let himself back inside his apartment.

He said goodnight to Terfle. 'Well, old watchbird, you're on duty now. We're not doing so badly for a couple of inexperienced amateurs.'

The open cigar box caught his eye.

'I take back my congratulations, Terfle. We won't be

graduating from the amateur league any time soon. Now what will I do with this?'

Then he spotted the tin of dried aphids.

'We'll just try the classic switcharoo,' he said.

He poured the aphids into an empty envelope, poured the sulphur crystals into the aphid tin, threw the crumpled newspapers into the trash, filled the cigar box with unpaid bills, and left it in plain sight on his desk. He wadded up all the wrapping paper and shoved it into his jacket pocket. He would drop it in the bin on the way to the shop in the morning. He looked around the study for any other telltale clues and found none.

He turned off the lights. Then stood for a moment by the window, peering out into the darkness. The street below was empty. The streetlight at the corner glowed reassuringly. Maybe he was being unnecessarily cautious.

But then again, maybe not.

Hermux brushed his teeth and combed his fur carefully. Then crawled into bed and took out his own journal.

He stared at the blank page for a long time. Then putting his pen firmly to it, he wrote

Thank you for unexpected surprises. Thank you for airmail. Thank you for gossipy postmice. Thank you for corner grocers. For sandwiches and honey fizz. For scary news and narrow escapes and trolleys and shopping-bags. Thank you for loyal pets and bold adventurers (and adventuresses). Thank you for hidden tribes and secret formulas and peculiar neighbours and snoopy reporters. Thank you for installation art. And snacks. And for a safe place to lay my head at night.

Chapter 40
BEGIN AT THE BEGINNING

The next morning Hermux was still switching on the lights when Pup arrived at the shop. He carried a large and rather heavy-looking paper bag.

'What a morning, Tantamoq!' exclaimed Pup, setting down his bag ceremoniously. 'Weather like this makes me feel like a new mole! Let's make news!'

'It looks like you made some progress at the newspaper morgue,' said Hermux, nodding towards the bag.

'Oh, no! This is progress of a different sort. Prink's progress I call it. A mixed dozen of Lanayda's freshest doughnuts. And two coffees. I wasn't sure how you take yours, so I got it with milk.'

'Oh,' said Hermux, happily sniffing the air. 'With milk is just fine. Let me get some saucers for our doughnuts. Pull up that stool, and we can eat at the counter.'

Minutes later the two of them were munching happily.

'You know, Tantamoq, maybe you can help me,' said Pup between bites.

'Mmmmph, I'd be glad to if I can.'

'Well, I can never decide whether it's her cinnamon-sugar or her coconut that's her best doughnut.'

'To be perfectly honest, Pup,' answered Hermux, sipping his strong coffee. 'I've never thought of it that way.'

He helped himself to a cinnamon-sugar and a coconut doughnut and proceeded to eat each of them. 'But I see what you mean. Personally I'm leaning towards the coconut. But the cinnamon-sugar does have a homey simplicity that's hard to beat. Perhaps it's a question that's best left undecided.'

'Like so many of the best questions,' agreed Pup. 'But now for the darker side of life. You asked me about Dr Mennus. I was able to dig up a little background for you. But first I need to ask you what's going on and what your involvement is. I warn you that Mennus is a nasty character. And if this is just idle curiosity on your part, I'd stay away from him.'

Hermux studied Pup carefully, and he decided he'd feel much better if he had somebody as smart and as competent as Pup on his side. He took a deep breath and began at the beginning.

Pup got out his notebook and began scribbling.

Hermux described Linka's visit to his shop.

'And you'd never met her before that afternoon?' asked Pup.

'Never set eyes on her. And I've only seen her once since then.' Hermux told about the arrival of the mysterious rat who had demanded Linka's watch. He told about following the rat to the offices of the Automated Laboratory Equipment Company.

'Nice work,' commented Pup, visibly impressed. 'And you're sure he didn't spot you?'

148

'Not a chance,' assured Hermux. 'And from there I tailed him all the way to Ms Perflinger's house. And that's where I got the number plate.'

'Ah, yes. The number plate. How vain! It may prove to be Mennus's undoing. And what exactly did you see at Ms Perflinger's?'

'Well, they came for her. And they escorted out of her house and into the car. She looked like she may have been drugged.'

'Who escorted her? Mennus himself?'

'Well, I have no idea. I don't know what he looks like.'

'Did he look like this?' asked Pup, taking an envelope from his jacket pocket and withdrawing a small handful of newspaper clippings. He unfolded the clippings and smoothed one out on the counter so Hermux could study it.

Hermux licked the cinnamon and sugar from his paw and took the clipping. It was a grainy black and white photo somewhat blurred and out of focus. It showed a silvery mole wearing dark glasses and a black beret. His smile, or his snarl (it was hard to tell), revealed a row of short, unnaturally sharp-looking teeth that gave him the appearance of a small shark with sleek fur.

'I didn't realize he was a mole,' said Hermux in surprise.

'What do you mean by that?' queried Pup in a somewhat irritated tone.

'I just mean I don't think of moles as criminals,' explained Hermux.

'Do you think we're not smart enough?' demanded Pup.

'Heavens, no! I mean, of course you are. But ... well, look at you, Pup. You're a very outgoing, civic-minded person.

149

You're involved in so many different aspects of city life. It's just hard to imagine someone like you as a criminal.'

'Well, not all moles are alike, Tantamoq. Just as not all mice are alike.'

'I see your point,' apologized Hermux. 'And the answer to your question then is that I did not see Mennus himself. He sent rats to do his dirty work.'

The phone rang noisily, and Hermux jumped.

'Hermux Tantamoq Watch and Clock Repair,' he answered.

There was no response.

Chapter 41
THE MYSTERIOUS DR MENNUS

'Is anyone there?' Hermux asked.

There was a click, and the line went dead. Hermux hung up the phone. It rang again immediately. He gave Pup a meaningful look. Then he picked up the receiver and fairly shouted into it, 'Whoever this is, stop these annoying calls immediately!'

A shrill voice pierced Hermux's ear. 'Nock! Hang up that extension! Right now! Mr Tantamoq, I'm so sorry. It's Cladenda Noddem. Nock's been playing with the phone. I was expecting you to phone about coming this morning. I wondered if you'd forgotten.'

'Oh, nibble it all! This is terrible! I completely forgot. I've been wrapped up in a ... in a very complicated repair, and the time has just flown. I hope I haven't inconvenienced you. If you'll be home later this morning, I'll come as soon as I can.'

'It's quite all right,' she reassured him. 'Nock is home from school with a cold. And we'll be here all day.'

'I'll be out just as soon as I finish this up,' said Hermux. 'And I'm sorry for snapping at you earlier. I'm just a bit on edge this week.'

'Don't worry,' she said as she hung up. 'We'll see you later.'

Pup pushed a jelly doughnut across the counter towards Hermux. 'You'd better have this, old mouse. You are acting a bit edgy this morning.'

Hermux took a small bite of doughnut and picked up the clipping and examined it again.

'The only photo I could find of the mysterious Dr Mennus, a.k.a. the Notorious Dr Mennus, a.k.a. the Beauty Doc, a.k.a. the Rat Shocker,' commented Pup. 'Notoriously camera shy.'

Hermux read the article that accompanied the photo.

PLASTIC SURGEON FIGHTS ELECTRO-SHOCK ALLEGATIONS

— Controversial beauty doctor Hiril Mennus denied malpractice charges filed against him today by actress Nurella Pinch. Miss Pinch claims Mennus's medical cruelty and gross negligence resulted in irreparable injury, as well as pain and suffering.

Pinch's charges stem from a course of rejuvenation therapy she underwent last year at the posh Youthanasia Spa operated by Dr Mennus.

At a news conference at Graffini Films headquarters, a studio spokesperson previewed sensational details of the forthcoming trial, including diagrams of bizarre-looking electro-shock instruments that Pinch claims were used in unauthorized 'experiments upon her person'.

Dr Mennus has vowed a vigorous legal defence. 'These Dr Frankenstein claims are preposterous. My rejuvenation therapy is a safe and proven success. I reverse the effects of ageing by stimulating the fur follicles with a gentle current of electricity that tones the underlying skin and restores the natural glossiness of the fur. Miss Pinch's ailments are completely unrelated to my therapy. She suffers unfortunately from an unstable personality aggravated by the condition of stardom, which has manifested itself in these regrettable symptoms of physical impairment.'

Miss Pinch, who has not been seen in public for more than a year, was not available for comment. Her publicist Dezra Balboney confirmed that Pinch will remain in seclusion for the foreseeable future. She would not comment on the extent of damage to Pinch's face and paws.

Miss Pinch, a perennial favourite with moviegoers around the world, catapulted to fame more than two decades ago in the ultra-successful *Beach Burrow Party* movies. A month ago her marriage to action film director Brinx Lotelle ended in divorce.

In recent months rumours of Pinch's deteriorating condition have circulated in the tightly knit film community.

According to an unidentified source at Graffini Films, the future of Ms Pinch's career is uncertain. 'Let's be blunt,' he stated. 'Her fur fell out. She's completely bald from the waist up.'

'That sounds horrible. When was this?' asked Hermux.

'Eight years ago.'

'What happened?'

'Mennus settled out of court. He lost Youthanasia. But he kept his medical licence.'

'And Nurella Pinch?'

'Dropped out of sight. Fairly eccentric. Still does some voice-overs. Books-on-tape. That sort of thing.'

'And Mennus?'

'Pulled up stakes. Moved to the Continent. Opened a sanitarium in the mountains. The usual rich clientele. The usual beauty procedures—haunch enhancements, snout reductions, claw removals. Pioneered the first pelt transplant four years ago. Moved back here two years ago with some significant bucks and opened the Last Resort. Kept a very low profile since then. But I do hear rumours.'

'What sort of rumours?'

'The usual sort—ungrateful patient, unfaithful employee. But no one ever files charges. And no one will talk to me. Never a word against the good doctor. But the looks! I get the strangest looks when I ask for an interview! Painful, faraway looks. That's why I'm convinced he's a tough customer. He's got some sort of eerie power over these people.'

Chapter 42
GETTING THE PICTURE

'And that's what I know about Mennus,' concluded Pup. 'Now what do you know?'

Hermux squirmed uncomfortably. 'What have you heard about the Millennium Project?' he asked.

'You mean Tucka Mertslin's new miracle cream?'

'I'm not sure what I mean really,' mused Hermux. 'It's all tied up with Ms Perflinger and her rescue mission for Dr Dandiffer's expedition in Teulabonari.'

'Whoa, there!' exclaimed Pup. 'You lost me. Dandiffer and Teulabonari and Tucka Mertslin and Mennus? What are you talking about?'

So Hermux explained about tasting the moon plant and how his whisker droop vanished overnight and how the moon plant vanished the next day. Then he told about intercepting Dandiffer's letter, and signing for the package, and arriving at the Perriflot Institute to meet Jervutz and finding that he had been murdered.

'You mean to tell me that you think Mennus was involved in Jervutz's death?'

'I don't know. I don't think it was a coincidence. Especially after reading Dandiffer's journal.'

'Dandiffer kept a journal?'

'Yes. It was in the package he sent.'

'And you have the journal?'

'Yes. And that's not all. I have the formula for eternal youth that he went to Teulabonari to get.'

Pup whistled in disbelief.

'Where are they?' he asked.

'I hid them,' Hermux told him.

'Where?'

'In a safe place.'

'How safe?'

'Very safe! Listen, I don't want to tell you where I hid them. I think it would be safer for you if you didn't know. At least for the time being. I've got to think this whole thing through.'

'All right. All right. So let's get back to the Perflinger dame.'

'Ms Perflinger!'

'Whatever. What happened after they took Ms Perflinger away?'

'Well, nothing. I haven't seen her. I called the police but they weren't interested.'

'You called the police?'

'Almost immediately. I told the sergeant what I'd seen, but he said that he couldn't arrest someone for getting into a limousine.'

'So he didn't buy the kidnapping routine?'

'It wasn't any routine. I was there. There wasn't anything routine about it!'

'Well, we've got to get more information before we can get

the police on board. What else do you know? Where does Mertslin fit in?'

'She's paying for Mennus's equipment. I heard her threaten him on the phone. He's working for her.'

'So the Beauty Doc and the Beauty Queen. There's a pretty pair for you. Have you got any proof? Anything on paper?'

'No. But Automated Laboratory Equipment would have the records.'

'Unfortunately there's nothing illegal about them working on research together. It doesn't add up to kidnapping or murder.'

'Don't you see?' asked Hermux. 'Dandiffer was working for Jervutz at the Perriflot Institute—searching for the youth serum in the jungle. Mennus planted a spy in Dandiffer's expedition. Jervutz found out about it and tried to warn him, and Mennus had him bumped off. It all fits! They're all after the Fountain of Youth!'

'And where does Perflinger fit in?'

'They must think she knows something about the formula.'

'So what do we do?'

'I don't know,' said a tired and disappointed Hermux.

Chapter 43
A PLAN TAKES SHAPE

A general aura of gloom settled over the shop. The coffee was cold. The doughnuts were gone. Hermux dipped the tip of his paw in a puddle of jelly and drew tiny circles on the counter-top.

Pup leaned back with his eyes closed and his feet propped against the safe. He sat up suddenly and slapped his leg.

'I've got it,' he exclaimed. 'I've got a plan!'

Hermux brightened considerably.

'What is it?' he asked.

'We've got to get inside Mennus's place and find Ms Perflinger ourselves. If we can, we'll get her out. And if we can't, we'll notify the police. But we'll get the proof we need to convince them first.'

'That's capital! A mole of action! That's what I like. How will it work?'

'I don't have all the details yet. But here it is roughly. You'll check into the clinic under an assumed name. I'll arrange it through the paper. Once you're situated, you'll search the place for Perflinger. In the meantime I'll work the lab equipment angle. I'll try to reach Dandiffer. And I'll do some digging around Perriflot and the Mertslin organization. We'll put all the pieces together, and if there's a case we'll make it. Of course, I'll have exclusive rights to the original story, ancillary rights, et cetera, et cetera ...'

'Of course,' said Hermux hesitantly. 'The main thing is that we'll get Ms Perflinger out of there before something dreadful happens to her.' He recalled the fate of poor Nurella Pinch, and he shuddered.

'Right!' said Pup with gusto. 'I'll get back to the office and get the wheels in motion. I'll call you this afternoon. Or this evening at the latest, and let you know what I've worked out. Get packed and ready to go. We've got to strike while the iron is hot!'

Chapter 44
A MONKEY'S WRENCH

It was nearly noon when Hermux rang the bell at Murt and Cladenda Noddem's stately brick home on Upper Thatchjigglin Lane. He brushed his whiskers absentmindedly as he waited.

Cladenda answered the door in a flour-smeared apron.

'Thank you for coming, Mr Tantamoq,' she smiled. 'Excuse the mess. Nock and I are baking biscuits. And I've made soup for lunch if you'd care to join us.'

Hermux wasn't hungry. But the mention of biscuits got his attention. 'Thank you, Mrs Noddem, but I've just eaten,' he fibbed. 'However, I will sample one of your biscuits later if I may.'

'Fine,' she said. 'I'll show you the clock, and let you get started. I'll be in the kitchen if you need me.'

Cladenda led him through the entrance hall and into the spacious living-room that adjoined it.

She had recently redecorated it, and she had chosen a floral motif. The room was wallpapered in broad bands of irises interwoven with garlands of marigolds. At the windows,

160

which looked out on to a formal garden, brilliant sprays of bouganvillaea and mounds of hot pink azaleas struggled to dominate the grass-green drapes. The enormous couch and the overstuffed chairs were upholstered in a matching chintz of yellow daisies floating in clouds of baby's breath. Great vases of lilacs covered the coffee table, the end tables, and the grand piano. And underfoot a bold rug of red and purple roses tied everything together with a vegetative force that made Hermux's head swim.

'I see you that you are fond of flowers,' stuttered Hermux.

'Oh, yes,' agreed Cladenda, spritzing the air generously with Spring Extravaganza Floral Room Deodorant by Tucka Mertslin. 'Enormously fond. I think they provide a positive, uplifting framework for our thoughts.'

Hermux felt his nose twitch in anticipation of a sneeze at the same time that his stomach gave an unpleasant lurch among the remains of the morning's six doughnuts.

'And with Nock at such an impressionable age,' continued Cladenda, 'I want to surround him with as much beauty as possible.'

'Quite right. And how is little Nock feeling now?' Hermux interjected. 'I trust that the thought of fresh biscuits has had a medicinal effect.'

'Oh! The biscuits!' she exclaimed. 'I must run before they burn.'

'Quite all right. I'll just go ahead and get started,' Hermux said, indicating the grandfather clock.

An hour later he had finished. Beauty evidently hadn't had much taming effect on Nock. And he had apparently grown bored with crimping pennies. Hermux found a ragged nickel

161

jammed into the big gear of the clock. It had bent the drive shaft, which Hermux replaced. Then he cleaned the whole clock mechanism. Judging by the handfuls of copper shavings Hermux removed, Nock may have earned more than enough from his crimped penny operation to pay for the repairs.

Hermux suddenly had the odd feeling that he was being watched. He pretended to rummage through his tool-case while he glanced furtively about the room. The door to the kitchen was opened just a crack, and he thought he spied a pair of small bright eyes observing him.

He finished oiling the clock's gears and bearings, reset the hands to one minute past one o'clock exactly, and pulled the weights up, and set the pendulum in motion. Then he stepped back and announced in a loud voice, 'Well, that does it! I can't do any more. One more problem with this clock and they'll have to bust it up with an axe and burn it. And what won't burn they'll have to sell for scrap iron. I wouldn't want to be the mouse that had to do that!'

He looked towards the kitchen door. It had quietly closed.

'And now I wonder about that biscuit,' he said with a grin.

Chapter 45
THE NEW LOOK

When Hermux opened the door to the shop he found a note that had been slipped under the door.

> *Great news, old mouse!*
> *It's all falling into place. You're registered at the clinic as Torvin L. Pulmix. Arriving on the late train tonight. The Last Resort limo will meet you at the station. You're a linoleum dealer from Couver. It's downstate in the hill country near the border. You've come to lose weight and recover from a nervous condition. You'll need a suitcase and new clothes. So go shopping this afternoon.*
> *I'll call tonight with more details.*
>
> *Pup*

'Shopping?' wondered Hermux out loud. 'I don't know what they're wearing in Couver. I've never even been to Couver. And I don't know anything about linoleum! Maybe this isn't such a good idea ...'

He looked at the clock. It was nearly 2.00 already. If he left now he could get the shopping done and maybe stop in a linoleum store and look around. And maybe on the way he could find time for lunch. The doughnuts and cookies were beginning to wear off.

He closed the shop again and scurried off in the direction of Orsik & Arrbale. The windows of the great department store were decorated for the summer season. Mouse families in matching plaid sunsuits were eating lavish picnics on matching plaid tablecloths laid out in a grassy field. Skinny otters in skimpy swimsuits were frolicking in front of luxurious riverbank apartments. Minks were lunching at tiny tables in chic pavement cafés. Rats in linen suits were racing motorscooters along sunlit country roads. Hermux was getting into the high spirits of it all until he turned the corner on to Villum Avenue and encountered a row of windows plastered over with white paper and covered with bold black block letters announcing the coming of Tucka Mertslin's Millennium.

Hermux scowled as he pushed his way through the revolving door and into the crowd on the main floor.

'Fresh mown hay?' asked a vivacious young chipmunk in a very tight pink dress.

'What?' asked Hermux in an irritated voice.

'Would you care to sample Fresh Mown Hay, the new sport fragrance from Reezor Bleesom? It's perfect for day and transitions well for summer evenings. It's made of natural oils and has no preservatives. It's an Orsik & Arrbale exclusive. Today's gift-with-purchase includes a beach tote and fur glistener. Would you care for a sample?' she repeated, waving a spray bottle towards his arm.

'No,' he said rather too forcefully. Then he reconsidered. 'Now that I remember it, I do need to get a little birthday gift for my cousin down in Couver. He runs a linoleum store there. Do you think he might wear something like this?'

'Oh, absolutely!' she told him. 'Fresh Mown Hay is perfect for a small town. It's a nice clean scent.'

She took Hermux's paw in a firm but friendly grip and sprayed twice on the inside of his wrist. It tickled.

'Not too assertive,' she continued breezily. 'But sophisticated in an understated way. It's designed for today's indoor/outdoor lifestyle.'

Hermux sniffed his wrist cautiously and couldn't resist smiling. It did smell like fresh mown hay. He recalled the mouse family picnicking in the store window and how carefree they looked in their plaid sunsuits. He felt a pang of envy.

'I'll take a bottle,' he said impulsively.

'I'm sure your cousin will be delighted. Shall I have it gift-wrapped?'

'That won't be necessary. He's very informal. But perhaps you could help me with something else. I'm going down to Couver for a few days, and I'd like to buy some clothes for the trip. I don't seem to have a very good feel for casual attire.'

She eyed his neatly-tailored, robin's-egg blue flannel suit, his egg-yolk yellow button-down shirt, his bow tie printed with tiny locomotives, and his natty brown oxfords.

'I see what you mean,' she said encouragingly. 'I think we can fix you up so you'll have no trouble fitting in.'

An hour and a half later a somewhat dazed Hermux prepared to exit the store. He carried a shopping-bag loaded with boxes and tissue-wrapped parcels in each hand.

'Good-bye, Mr Tantamoq,' trilled the helpful young saleswoman. 'I hope your visit is a wonderful success. And thank you for shopping at Orsik & Arrbale.'

Hermux's stomach grumbled noisily as he pushed his way again through the revolving door. In all the rush and excitement he still hadn't eaten lunch. Out on the street he checked his watch. Too late for lunch. Too early for dinner.

If he hurried, he could make it to Lanayda's before she closed. Maybe she still had a doughnut or two left.

Chapter 46
CLOTHES MAKE THE MOUSE

Hermux was out of breath with excitement when he rushed into his apartment.

'I'll be there in just a minute,' he called merrily to Terfle. 'I've got a surprise!'

He scurried down the hall to his bedroom and emptied the contents of his shopping bags on the floor. 'Country Club Luau?' or 'Courthouse Casual?' muttered Hermux as he rummaged frantically through the pile. 'Definitely the luau,' he decided. 'Terfle will appreciate the colour.'

He removed his suit and hung it in the wardrobe. He stepped into a pair of baggy nylon shorts the colour of freshly cut watermelon with large turquoise polka dots. The salesgirl had recommended an elastic waist for comfort. He turned sideways and took a good look at himself in the mirror. He was looking a trifle plumpish, and he wondered if Pup was serious about his needing to lose weight. Hermux sucked in his stomach and slipped on an oversized Hawaiian shirt and buttoned it up. He particularly liked the shirt, with its iridescent green parrots in flight across a tropical beach at sunset.

He opened a shoebox and put on the thick plastic sandals the colour of a new daffodil that the salesgirl had told him tied everything together. She had paired them with thick cranberry and orange striped socks and had showed him how to roll them down to create thick cuffs above the sandals. 'The whole look says Country Club,' she had announced triumphantly.

Hermux added the furry crushable hat that matched the orange in the socks and beamed at himself in the mirror.

'It's an entirely new me,' he boasted. 'Ready for an entirely new adventure.'

He marched proudly to the study, warning Terfle in advance, 'Close your eyes until I tell you.'

If he hadn't been so excited, Hermux would have noticed that something was amiss the first moment he had unlocked his front door. If he hadn't been preoccupied with the lingering fragrance of Fresh Mown Hay that still clung so pleasantly to him, his sensitive nose would have picked up the scent of a stranger and the traces of fresh air that wafted in from the broken window in the study. He wouldn't have been so shocked by the chaos of ransacked papers, the wildly strewn books and the furniture in disarray that greeted his eye when he leapt wildly through the door of the study and shouted, 'Surprise!'

He would have known already that Terfle's cage had been overturned; that the door of the cage had been knocked open; and that Terfle was gone.

Chapter 47
DEAR DEPARTED FRIEND

'Surprise?' he repeated in a small, defeated voice. He turned slowly and surveyed the wreckage. He stopped at Terfle's cage.

'Terfle?' he asked hopefully. 'Where are you?'

There was no answer.

He ran to the cage and knelt beside it. It was empty. A cool spring breeze blew in through the broken window above. Hermux examined the floor around the cage. There was no sign of Terfle in the shards and fragments of broken glass. He righted the cage on its stand.

'Terfle, old friend! It's okay. I'm home now. You can come out! Wherever you're hiding. It's safe. You can come out!'

The room was silent.

Hermux rushed through the apartment looking for her. She was not in the kitchen. She was not in the bathroom. She was not in the hall. Terfle was gone.

Hermux walked back to the study and stood in front of the broken window.

'Oh, Terfle!' he cried. 'Please come back. Don't disappear on me! Please.'

He wiped a tear from his eye. And then another. Then he collapsed wearily on the floor, a small grey mouse dressed up for a summer holiday. And he sobbed bitterly.

Chapter 48
THE KING OF TEULABONARI

Hermux sat motionless and downcast amidst the wreckage of his study. Dusk deepened into darkness. The lights came on in the streets below. Finally he stood up and wiped his eyes. He stood and looked out into the empty night. Lit by the orange glow of the streetlights, his face was set in a fierce mask.

He raised an angry fist to the black sky.

'Mennus,' he muttered. 'I know you're behind this. And as sure as corn is sweet and cheese goes mouldy in the rain, I'll see that you pay for this. And pay dearly!'

He switched on the lights and took stock of the damage.

The burglar had climbed the fire escape, broken the window, and unlocked it. It looked like he, or she, had upset Terfle's cage as they came through the window. Everything in the room had been opened, turned out, turned up, and turned over.

Hermux remembered the youth formula. He slid open the cage bottom and lifted up the newspaper. The formula was still there.

He telephoned the police.

'This is Hermux Tantamoq. I'd like to report a burglary and a missing person.'

'Tantamoq, huh? Sounds vaguely familiar,' said a vaguely familiar voice. 'Right! This time you think it's a burglary, huh?'

'I don't think it was a burglary,' retorted Hermux. 'It was a burglary. My window is broken. My study is a mess. And Terfle is missing.'

'What was stolen?'

'Well, it doesn't appear that anything was stolen.'

'Right. Nothing was stolen. Then I'm afraid you can't report a Burglary. For a Burglary you need stolen property. Let me see ... maybe you could report a Breaking and Entering. If your window actually was broken. And if someone really entered the premises.'

'Well, of course the window was broken! How else would they have got in?'

'Right. Reporting a B&E at 7.45 p.m. And a missing person. Who is it this time?'

'It's Terfle. My pet ladybird,' Hermux explained. 'Her cage was knocked over. She must have flown out the open window. She'll be very confused out there. It's dark. She could be killed.'

'Say!' interrupted the sergeant. 'This is the police. Not the Rodentine Society. If you want to report a missing pet, I suggest you call them.'

'All right. All right. Just send out a police car!'

'A police car?' snorted the sergeant. 'For a burglar that didn't take anything? Listen, Mr Tantamink. If I can spare anyone, I'll send somebody out next week to take a statement.

And while it seems like you've got nothing better to do than call me up with girlfriends riding around in limousines and pet ladybirds flying around outside at night, I've got work to do. I've got my hands full with the Jervutz murder. And not a lead in sight.'

'But I know who killed Dr Jervutz!' exclaimed Hermux.

'Right! And I'm the King of Teulabonari!' snapped the sergeant and hung up.

Chapter 49
TIME TO GO!

'Well, we're on our own now!' said Hermux, and then he caught himself. There was no one there to hear him.

The telephone rang.

'Tantamoq? Are you packed and ready?' It was Pup. Hermux was relieved to hear a friendly voice on the line.

'No. Not packed,' said Hermux. 'There's been a problem!'

'No time now! Tell me about it in the cab! I'll be by to pick you up in twenty minutes.'

'Twenty minutes? I can't be ready in twenty minutes!'

But Pup had already rung off.

Hermux gave up on straightening the study. He ran to the bedroom and dragged his suitcase down from the top of the wardrobe.

He changed out of his Luau clothes and into the Courthouse Casual, a pink and white striped shirt, a lime green cardigan sweater, and bright blue seersucker trousers. Then he threw the remainder of his new clothes into the suitcase.

He retrieved his toothbrush, his fur brush and his comb

from the bathroom. He gathered up toothpaste and shampoo and a jar of Flip wax.

From his bureau he counted out four pairs of underwear, four T-shirts, and four pairs of socks—just in case. He took his journal from its place on the bedside table. He found his reading glasses in the rubble of books and magazines by his chair in the study.

He stopped to catch his breath, and the front door buzzer sounded.

'Who is it?' he asked into the intercom.

'It's Pup! The cab's here!'

'I'll be right down.'

Hermux closed the suitcase and checked himself hurriedly in the mirror. He tried to look breezy and nonchalant. But he only succeeded in looking disoriented.

'What if it turns cold?' he thought. He grabbed his old jacket from the hook by the front door, reopened his suitcase and managed to squeeze it inside.

It wasn't until he got to the elevator that he remembered that Terfle was missing. And then he felt doubly terrible. First that she was gone. And second that he had forgotten her.

He ran back inside the apartment. He refilled her water bowl and her food bowl. He scattered a handful of dried aphids on the window ledge and poured a line of them that led back inside the window.

'If she comes back,' he thought as he re-locked the door. Then he corrected himself. 'When she comes back!'

Chapter 50
BIG YELLOW TAXI

The Night Owl taxicab was waiting at the curb. Pup threw open the door and helped Hermux load his suitcase in.

'The train station!' Pup told the driver. 'And step on it!'

As the taxi sped off through the empty streets of the city, Pup lowered his voice to a whisper and spoke rapidly to Hermux.

'Everything's set! Go down to the track and act like you just arrived on the train from Couver. The car will pick you up in front of the station and drive you out to the Last Resort. Check in and get a good night's sleep. Incidentally you look awful. Just right for someone on the edge of a nervous breakdown. Tomorrow try to get a look around the clinic. If you see anything suspicious call me at this number.' Pup gave Hermux a scrap of paper with a telephone number scrawled on it.

'It rings straight through to me. Use the pay phone. There should be one in the lobby. If I find anything out I'll call you. I'll say that it's the linoleum store calling and that we're having a problem finding an item in stock. That will be your signal to call me at this number. Don't lose it.'

The brick clocktower of the Pinchester Central train station loomed up out of the night.

'Here we are. Go around to the side entrance,' Pup instructed the driver. Hermux crawled out of the cab, and Pup handed him out his suitcase.

'All right!' said Pup cheerily. 'Take care of yourself!' He extended his paw, and the two friends shook hands warmly.

The cab pulled away from the kerb. Pup rolled down his window and leaned out. 'Give it your best, old mouse!' he called to Hermux and waved a bold goodbye.

Hermux watched the taxi until it turned a corner and disappeared. Then he took up his suitcase and slipped quietly into the train terminal.

Chapter 51
A WARM RECEPTION

The big clock in the deserted waiting-room said 8.42. Hermux checked his watch. It was 8.38.

'Tsk! Tsk!' he said. 'And it's a train station. I had no idea things had gotten this bad.'

He checked the arrivals board. The train from Couver was due to arrive at 8.45 on Track 7, and it was due on time. Hermux hurried off in search of Track 7. When he got there he found a handful of people already waiting to meet it.

A group of porters arrived and began pushing their carts into position to offload the incoming luggage and freight. Hermux took up an inconspicuous position behind a cart. He set his suitcase down and peered down the tracks. The flashing headlight of the old streamlined locomotive was just coming into view. Within moments the platform vibrated with the deep rumbling purr of the engines, and the melancholy smell of diesel hung in the air.

As the tired-looking passengers stepped down from the train and looked about them for friends and family, Hermux moved forward and tried to blend in and give the impression that he too was tired from the long ride up from Couver. Then like a sleepy, overfed snake the whole crowd began to move slowly towards the station. Hermux scanned the scene nervously. Just inside the station doors stood the white rat who had driven the car when Linka was kidnapped. He held a small sign that read:

The Last Resort
Welcomes
Mr Pulmix

Even in his chequered green chauffeur's uniform the rat looked shifty and sneaky. Maybe it was his red eyes. Or the way he held his cigarette between the two middle claws of his paw. Or the hungry way he studied the passengers.

It took Hermux a long moment to remember that he was Mr Pulmix. He set down his suitcase and waved at the rat.

The rat tossed his cigarette on the marble floor and stubbed it out with the toe of his high-heeled boot. Hermux held out his hand in greeting. The rat ignored him.

'Just the one bag?' he asked Hermux coldly.

'Yes. I've just got the one,' Hermux apologized.

'Not much for a long stay,' the rat said as he lifted the bag.

'I don't really intend a very long stay.'

'Yeah, that's what they all say,' the rat answered. 'The car's out in front.'

Chapter 52
GREAT EXPECTATIONS

The limousine was powerful and fast. And the rat was a good driver. In minutes they had left the city behind them and were heading west on the old highway that followed the river. The headlights cut through the darkness like a straight razor. Beside them the river was a winding ribbon of blackness touched here and there by fingers of moonlight.

They passed through a sleepy, shuttered village and turned off the highway on to a country road. The road led beneath the ruin of an old railroad bridge whose broken stone piers loomed above them in a cruel smile.

Then the road rose quickly from the river valley to a broad plateau of hayfields and apple orchards. The fields and orchards gradually gave way to thick pine woods, and the road began to descend again.

A veil of mist crept up from the valley below them and gradually thickened into dense, blinding fog. But the rat did not slow the car. He dimmed the headlights and plunged forward at breakneck speed. In the back seat Hermux clung to the door handle and peered anxiously out the window.

Suddenly the limousine lurched off the road and skidded on to a gravel drive of some sort.

A large sign flashed by them framed by marble columns and brightly lit by spotlights.

THE LAST RESORT
Health Spa and Research Clinic
Your host
Hiril Mennus, M.D.
Cosmetic Surgeon

'For the Rest of Your Life'

A massive iron gate materialized in the fog. The driver stopped and rolled down his window.

'Mr Pulmix arriving from Couver,' he announced to someone inside the gate. After a long moment Hermux heard the jangle of keys and the click of a well-oiled lock. The gates swung slowly open before them.

The limousine rolled slowly through the entrance and then picked up speed again. Hermux turned with a lump in his throat and watched the gates close firmly behind them.

The drive entered a long curving avenue of sycamore trees and then came out at the edge of what seemed like an enormous lawn. There, brightly lit and hovering above the fog like a weightless apparition, stood the Last Resort.

Hermux gasped.

It was a lot bigger than he had expected. It was whiter, and chillier, and more isolated. And well, it was just plain scarier all around.

'This is for Ms Perflinger,' he thought to steady himself.

The rat cruised to a stop beneath the broad portico of the main building and killed the engine.

A stern-looking hamster in a sleek white nurse's uniform descended the broad steps and opened the door of the limousine.

'Welcome to the Last Resort,' she told Hermux. 'We've been expecting you.'

Chapter 53
NATURE'S TONIC

'Take Mr Pulmix's luggage to the Ivy Bungalow,' the nurse told the white rat. 'And put that cigarette out! You know the rules. No smoking anywhere on the grounds. If I catch you again, I'll report you to Mennus.'

'That's right! Tell the doctor,' hissed the rat. 'One of these days nice nursey may get a nasty little shock!' He took a long drag on his cigarette and flipped the butt at the nurse's feet.

The nurse glared at the rat. Then snorted dismissively. She took Hermux by the elbow and led him up the steps and into the reception lobby. It was a grand modern room. Banks of tall glass doors opened out along two sides on to a deep verandah that circled the building. A fountain in the form of a monumental painted teapot dominated the room. Water poured from the spout over a cascade of teacups that spilled merrily into an enormous saucer below. A school of goldfish swam lazily about the saucer.

Hermux was delighted. There must have been more than a hundred teacups that moved back and forth in the streaming water emptying and filling. Each one was a different pattern. He couldn't see any mechanism.

The nurse crossed to the reception desk and stepped behind it. She opened a file and spread it on the counter.

'Torvin L. Pulmix. Here for the rest cure, I see.' She fixed a hard eye on him and arched an eyebrow. 'And weight loss.'

Hermux nodded nervously.

'The arrangements were rather sudden,' she said. 'Only this afternoon.'

'Yes,' he stuttered. 'I decided on the spur of the moment. I've been under enormous pressure the last few months. We're in the middle of a building boom down in Couver. I keep thinking I'll slow down and take a little vacation, but the demand for linoleum just keeps skyrocketing. About two weeks ago I found I could no longer get my mind off of it. Linoleum, I mean. You see I think about it all the time. I dream about it. Great waves of linoleum in the most durable and attractive finishes. When I close my eyes, I see exotic new linoleum patterns. When I open them, I see a whole new world of uses for linoleum.'

Hermux stopped to catch his breath. The nurse peered at him warily over her half-glasses. Hermux looked around the lobby admiringly. 'And may I say that your lobby would look very grand in our newest Candy-cane-and-Snowflake pattern. Very grand indeed. It's very popular now. And I could offer you a very competitive price.'

'If you will look carefully, Mr Pulmix, you will see that our floor is an exquisitely rare imported marble. I hardly think that linoleum would be an appropriate replacement. In any case, it's late, and you must be very tired after your journey.

You'll want to get an early start tomorrow on your rest cure.'

'I was thinking that I'd like to sleep in tomorrow,' responded Hermux, who was in fact beginning to feel like he could use a rest cure. A real one.

'Nonsense,' she chided him. 'You'd miss the most restful part of the day. Our programme begins at 6.00 a.m. sharp. Your personal rest consultant will call for you. Morning callisthenics. A light breakfast. Then your initial evaluation. Programme design. Programme implementation. It's going to be a very busy morning for you. I'd suggest getting right to bed. The porter will show you to your bungalow.'

'You mean I won't be staying in the main building?'

'Of course not. The main building houses the treatment facilities,' she explained, indicating the door to the left of her desk. 'And Dr Mennus's research laboratories,' she continued, gesturing towards the door to her right. It was marked:

Restricted Area
Absolutely No Entrance

'Each of our guests is housed in a private bungalow with all the amenities of a luxurious home. I'm sure you'll find yours very comfortable.

'If you should need anything in the night don't hesitate to call. There's always someone here at the front desk.'

'And my key?'

'There is no key, Mr Pulmix,' she explained. 'In the words of Dr Mennus, 'Trust is nature's beauty tonic.' We encourage our guests to move beyond their personal anxieties and open themselves to the healthful influences of a community of good intentions. There are no locks in our guest quarters. They're simply not necessary.'

'Isn't that a lock on the door to the laboratories?' inquired Hermux who had been studying the sturdy-looking, steel door.

'Those are not guest quarters,' she answered condescendingly. 'You needn't concern yourself with the laboratories. Scientific research is an altogether different proposition from health or beauty. Different rules apply. Your job while you're with us is simply to relax and take full advantage of our complete range of innovative health and beauty resources. And now if there is nothing else, I'll ring for a porter. Have a pleasant night's sleep.'

Chapter 54
HITHER AND SLITHER

The porter, an elderly gopher, led the way to the Ivy Bungalow holding a kerosene lantern in his somewhat shaky paw.

'Well,' offered Hermux enthusiastically. 'It's certainly a beautiful place, the Last Resort!'

'Depends on whether you're coming or going,' answered the porter.

'I'm just coming, of course,' Hermux went on. 'It seems very impressive.'

'Not much to see in the dark.'

'No. But what there is is lovely.'

'Some think so. Some don't.'

'I'm certainly looking forward to meeting the famous Dr Mennus,' added Hermux hopefully.

'Not likely.'

'Is he away from the clinic?'

'Busy,' mumbled the porter. He stopped briefly and pointed towards the rear of the main building where lights shone brightly from the windows on the ground floor. 'In the lab.'

'It must be fascinating to watch him work. I'd love to visit the laboratory while I'm here.'

'Off limits!'

'Well, certainly,' sputtered Hermux. 'I only meant that ...'

'Ivy Bungalow,' interrupted the gopher, opening the front door and motioning Hermux inside. 'Bedroom. Bathroom. Sitting area,' he announced mechanically, pointing out the basic features of the cottage. 'Breakfast at 6.30.' He tapped a worn black claw on the small, framed map next to the door. 'Main dining-room.'

Hermux drew open the curtains on the front window and looked out across the darkness towards the lights coming from Mennus's laboratory.

'Wandering around at night's not a good idea,' advised the porter. 'Snakes.'

Hermux shuddered. The porter stared blankly at him, apparently in no hurry to go back out into the darkness.

'Snakes?' wheezed Hermux.

'Mennus keeps 'em,' the gopher explained. 'Security.' He still made no move to leave.

Finally Hermux realized that he expected a tip. He dug urgently in the pockets of his bright blue seersucker trousers and found three quarters. 'Here you are!' he told the gopher. 'And thank you!'

The gopher accepted the tip without comment. From the depths of his overalls he extracted a small leather change purse, snapped it open, deposited the coins inside, returned the purse to its hiding place, and then left without saying another word.

Hermux closed the door behind him and latched it. But

188

there was no lock. Not even a safety chain. The thought of snakes patrolling the grounds was horrifying to Hermux. The first thing he did was push the desk from the sitting area in front of the door and stack the hassock on top of it. He closed the curtains again, first making sure the window was firmly latched.

Then he looked around. The Ivy Bungalow was very pretty with ivy wallpaper, twig furniture, and a cheerful blaze in the small stone fireplace. He knew he should pay close attention to his surroundings.

But Hermux didn't really care. He was exhausted. He was frightened. He was worried. And he was alone.

He turned down the bed and put on his pyjamas. He brushed his teeth and brushed his fur. Then he got into bed and opened his journal.

It had been a long and confusing day. There was a lot to say, and he didn't have much energy left for the effort.

> Thank you, he wrote
> for good friends like Pup. And Terfle.

He closed his eyes a moment and thought of Terfle. She was alone somewhere out there in the night. And she probably didn't have a cosy bungalow, or a soft bed, or a fire to cheer her up. Or, hopefully, a snake on patrol outside her window.

> Thank you for hope. For lights in windows. For finding the way home. Thank you for the scent of fresh mown hay. For picnics. For sunsuits. For moonlit rivers, and apple orchards, and foggy drives. Thank you for doughnuts. And locks on doors.

And with that he jumped up from his bed and pushed the

desk even more tightly against the front door. He carried a stack of books over from the bookcase and piled them on top of the hassock. Then he crawled back into bed, turned off the bedside lamp, and fell into a deep sleep.

Chapter 55
HEALTHY CHOICES

Sunlight poured through the window next to Hermux's bed and woke him long before the alarm clock. He stayed in bed thinking through what lay ahead of him. Today he must set about discovering the whereabouts of Ms Perflinger without arousing any suspicions. He couldn't very well ask at the front desk where she was being kept prisoner.

'I'll bet it's the laboratory,' he said to himself. 'I've got to see if I can get inside.'

Then he roused himself because he was feeling ever so hungry. While he showered, he imagined the breakfast that was waiting for him in the main dining-room. Buckwheat pancakes for sure. With real maple syrup. Hot buttered toast spread with a thick layer of clover jam. Fresh raspberry juice. A chunk of gooey breakfast cheese with sesame crisp. And a fat steaming pot of coffee all for himself. With real cream.

He pulled on a golden yellow turtleneck sweater, stepped into his new cherry red corduroy overalls, and set off for the main building.

Bathed in the fresh morning light the Last Resort wasn't

191

the least bit gloomy or sinister. It was a spacious park of sparkling lawns, immaculately trimmed hedges, and broad, winding pathways. Immediately outside the Ivy Bungalow was a sign. The swimming-pool was to the right. The dining-room was to the left. The spa was straight ahead. It was a friendly, inviting place. Hermux's spirits rose and he turned to the left and quickened his pace towards breakfast.

The dining-room was already quite crowded when Hermux arrived.

A young ground squirrel in a crisp plaid uniform conducted Hermux to a small table set for one. She rushed off before he could order coffee. While he waited for her to return Hermux surveyed the dining-room and the other guests.

The setting was impressive. A lush tangle of painted trees and foliage covered the walls. White lattice columns supported a series of magnificent wisteria vines that rose up to the ceiling and then joined together trailing dense masses of wisteria blossoms. A warm lavender glow enveloped the space. Hermux was delighted.

'This is certainly beautiful,' he told himself with satisfaction. As he stared at the wisterias he realized that they were not real but artificial. The wisterias were in fact an enormous chandelier. The warm lavender light emanated from the blossoms. It was a very pleasant effect.

When the waitress returned with the menu, he noticed immediately that she looked particularly fetching in the light. In fact as he looked around at the other guests they all looked unexpectedly youthful and fresh.

Except for the woman seated at the table next to him, whose face and paws were completely swathed in bandages.

'I'll take a cup of coffee right away if you don't mind,' Hermux told the waitress.

'We don't serve coffee at the Last Resort. It dulls the fur. I can offer you alfalfa stem, buttercup, or columbine tea.'

'No coffee at all?' asked Hermux with a sinking heart. It was one thing to be all alone and facing certain death or worse at the hands of Dr Mennus, and it was another thing to be expected to do it without coffee. 'All right, then,' he said. 'I guess I'll have the buttercup tea. But make it strong.'

He snapped open his menu and stared at it in dumbfounded silence. He expected pages and pages of bright pictures of pancakes of every variety shown in plain stacks, or built into castles or bridges or igloos, or shaped like aeroplanes, or rowboats or fire engines. And pitchers of syrup to choose from—partridge berry syrup, thimbleberry syrup, huckleberry syrup, boysenberry syrup, and raspberry syrup. Then there would be cheese plates and cheeses à la carte. Creamy cheeses, crumbly cheeses, and peculiar little cheeses in peculiar little clay pots.

But there was none of that.

Hermux's eyes narrowed into a nasty frown as he studied the menu, which had no pictures at all.

Hermux felt close to tears. It didn't seem quite fair. After such a difficult week and with unknown dangers still ahead of him, there was not so much as a day-old doughnut to get him through the morning.

'I'd stay away from the fern root if I were you. It's overcooked.'

Hermux looked up. The woman in bandages had put down her magazine and was speaking to him. Dark brown

193

Menu

The Root Course
Braised Bracken Fern Root in Yarrow Sauce
or
Meadow Melange
Coarsely chopped radishes, parsnips, and hearts of elm.
Mustard/clover salsa. Served at room temperature.

Herb du Jour
Marinated Dandelion Buds on a bed of Baby Forest Greens
(wood-sorrel, chicory, and vetch)

Fresh-baked breads
Bran sticks with Figwort Jelly
Oat thins with Turnip Pâté de Campagne

Cucumber and Lima Bean Sherbet

Freshly Squeezed Juices
Milkweed
Thistle
Potato

Chef Bussy Gloomper

eyes twinkled out through small slits in the snow-white gauze that wrapped her head. She lifted a pink plastic straw to another slit and sipped demurely at a pale green liquid in a tall fluted glass.

'What would you suggest?' he asked, trying not to stare rudely.

'The herb du jour,' she told him. 'I still can't chew anything. But it smells heavenly. Of course the breads are

194

grotesquely fattening, but why not live it up? A little nip and tuck and Mennus will have you as slim as a churchmouse again.'

She picked up her issue of *Décor Deluxe* and began to read.

On the cover was a photograph of Tucka Mertslin and Rink Firsheen laughing together in the demolished lobby of Hermux's building.

Tucka Burrows In!

'Drat that woman!' scowled Hermux. 'She's inescapable!'

'Have you decided on breakfast?' asked the waitress, who had returned for Hermux's order.

'Well, yes,' said Hermux thoughtfully. 'I think I'll have ...' And he was about to ask for the herb du jour, two orders of the bran sticks with figwort jelly, and a extra-tall glass of potato juice when a stern voice rang out above the noise of the dining-room.

'Torvin L. Pulmix! Preliminary examination! In the main examination room! Step lively!'

A momentary hush fell over the guests.

Hermux spied a stout, middle-aged mouse in a white pantsuit standing at the top of the entrance stairs. She carried a large clipboard which she tapped impatiently with her pen.

'Guest Pulmix? Torvin L. Pulmix?' she repeated even more loudly. 'Preliminary exam and evaluation!'

'Oh!' gasped Hermux leaping to his feet. 'That's me! But I haven't eaten anything yet!'

Chapter 56
THE NAKED TRUTH

'Take off all your clothes and step on the scale,' the nurse/evaluator told him matter-of-factly as she unwound a coil of measuring tape.

Hermux waited for her to leave the examining room.

'Well?' she snapped. 'I haven't got all day. I have other guests to evaluate. Let's get a move on!'

Hermux still hesitated. He looked around for a robe, or a sheet, or a towel. There was nothing. He studied the name-tag pinned securely to the nurse's stately bosom.

Korralinch Tarmon, R.N.
Director of Medical Evaluations

'Is there a problem, Mr Pulmix?' she asked. 'Because if there is a problem I can speak to Dr Mennus right now ...'

Hermux flinched.

'No,' he said, resigned to his fate. 'I'm just not accustomed to undressing in public.'

'This isn't public, Mr Pulmix. It's quite private. There's

only you and me. And I am a licensed and experienced health professional. You can hardly expect the clinic to assume responsibility for your return to robust health without our conducting a thorough examination before we begin. The liabilities would be unspeakable.'

'Certainly,' agreed Hermux. 'The liabilities would be unspeakable.'

Hermux removed his blue rubber clogs and pulled off his orange argyle socks. He unsnapped his cherry-red corduroy overalls and stepped out of them. He pulled his golden-yellow turtleneck over his head. And stood there in his flannel boxer shorts printed all over with furry black bumblebees.

He paused. Nurse Tarmon rapped irritably on her clipboard.

Hermux closed his eyes and dropped his shorts. He stepped on to the scale and stood there miserably.

Nurse Tarmon clicked the scale weights into place.

'Tsk! Tsk!' she remarked disapprovingly. 'Just as I suspected.'

The tape-measure was thrown loosely around Hermux's waist. Hermux held his stomach in bravely. He felt a sharp jab in the ribs and let it go only for a moment. But Nurse Tarmon was too fast for him. She tightened the measuring tape.

'Tsk! Tsk!' she repeated. 'Not good. Climb up on this.' She pointed to a small stool and took out a stopwatch.

Hermux climbed up on the stool.

'Now jump down. And climb back up,' she told him. 'And keep doing that until I tell you to stop.'

Hermux jumped down. He climbed back up. He jumped down. He climbed back up again. He kept doing that until finally she clicked the stopwatch and said, 'Stop!'

Hermux was breathing heavily and his heart was pounding. She listened to both with a stethoscope.

Hermux closed his eyes again and stood there with his eyes tightly closed. He could hear her writing furiously on her clipboard. Then there was a sudden flash of light.

Hermux opened his eyes in time to see a piece of film pop out of an instant camera in Nurse Tarmon's hands.

'Just a medical record,' she told him brusquely. She watched the picture develop for a minute with a disapproving expression on her face. Then she crossed to her desk and dropped the film into a large envelope.

'You can dress now, Mr Pulmix. I'm afraid we have some serious work ahead of us!'

Chapter 57
IN THE ZONE

The calliope organ belched great puffs of steam into the hazy, overheated air of the gymnasium. Looking out over the churning sea of exercise equipment, the calliope player shouted into his microphone, 'Now step it up! Step it up!' And he doubled his marching tempo into a galloping frenzy that drove the aerobic enthusiasts to new heights of exertion. Hermux leapt forward, transported by the wild energy of the music. He drove his exercise wheel faster and faster until it vanished in a blur of whirring steel and sweaty fur.

'Cool down!' shouted the calliopist, swinging seamlessly into a slow, lilting waltz. Hermux slowed his pace. He huffed and puffed. His chest pounded. His legs ached. The wheel spun slowly to a stop, and Hermux staggered off. He saw spots before his eyes. He grabbed his towel and mopped his face.

'Gosh!' he gasped. 'I'm exhausted. I hope we eat soon. And I'd like to take a nap.'

But from the look on Nurse Tarmon's face as she threaded her way through the crowd towards him, that was not to be.

'Mr Pulmix,' she said. 'I'm glad I caught you. Luckily

we've had a cancellation. I've scheduled you for a complete pelt. Report to Treatment Room 3 immediately.'

She handed him an appointment card.

'Do you think I have time to eat before then?' he asked hopefully.

'Not possible,' she chided him. 'And I'm just coming from a consult with your nutritionist. I don't think lunch is in your future any time soon. We'll be going over the entire programme with you this afternoon. We're putting you on Special Diet. No more of that rich Dining Room food for you.'

'But I haven't even tasted it yet,' complained Hermux.

'All the better for you, dear,' she told him with a wink. 'What you don't put on now, you won't have to take off later.'

Hermux sighed.

'Now you'd better get a move on if you're going to make your pelt appointment. It's not a good idea to keep Hutt waiting.'

Chapter 58
POOR PROGNOSIS

Scaffolo Hutt, licensed cosmetologist and board certified pelt specialist, gestured towards the treatment chair.

'Please sit down, Mr Pulmix,' he said in a resonant voice with a barely detectable foreign accent. 'I've just been examining your chart. It's most interesting. I wonder if you've recently suffered from a nervous shock?'

'A shock?' asked Hermux. 'Well, now that you mention it, I've had several shocks in the past few weeks. I haven't been sleeping well. You see linoleum, which is what I'm in, is a very volatile business.'

'Hmmm,' responded Hutt, adjusting a bright light. 'Now just relax.' He depressed a foot pedal on the chair and the chair slid comfortably down until Hermux found himself lying on his back staring up into Hutt's face through an enormous magnifying-glass.

Hermux had never seen a sable so close up before. 'They certainly have impressive teeth,' he thought to himself. 'And their fur, if he's any example, is extremely thick and silky.'

Indeed, each hair on Scaffolo Hutt's head seemed infused

with light–blue-black at the roots, with flecks of gold at the tips. It was so rich and luxurious looking that Hermux was tempted to reach up and pat Hutt's head to see if it was real.

'Hmmm,' said Hutt. 'Some atrophy of the sebaceous glands. Nothing serious. Overall dryness. To be expected.'

He combed through Hermux's fur with a fine metal comb. 'Some flaking. No evidence of parasites.'

'Parasites?' demanded Hermux. 'What do you mean?'

Hutt grabbed a handful of fur at Hermux's neck and yanked it vigorously.

'Ouch!' squawked Hermux.

'Adequate follicle vigour.'

He plucked a single hair from Hermux's head and measured its thickness with small calipers.

Then he placed it in a microscope and studied it.

'Regular scale pattern. Acceptable density. Somewhat porous.' He wrote at some length on Hermux's chart.

Then he returned Hermux to an upright position and snapped off the light.

'I think that what we're dealing with here is a somewhat advanced case of chronic mid-life drabness. Luckily it can still be treated. At this late state I suggest an aggressive approach.'

'Drabness?' asked Hermux in a shocked tone. 'I've never thought of myself as drab.'

'Chronically drab,' Hutt corrected. 'But treatable. You've got to focus on that now.'

He scribbled several lines on his treatment pad, tore the sheet off and handed it to Hermux.

'Give this to my assistant,' Hutt told him. 'We should start immediately.'

Chapter 59
AN INVITATION

Hermux lay like a corpse on the couch in front of the fireplace. His eyes were glazed. His breathing barely perceptible. Slowly he raised a gloved hand and looked at his watch. He was relieved to see that there was still a half-hour before dinner. As hungry as he was, he hurt too much to even begin to think about showering, dressing, and walking all the way over to the main dining-room.

He turned on to his back and stared miserably at the ceiling. A sharp pain in his ribs reminded him of the long afternoon he had spent at the Suppleness Centre getting the first of the series of three deep preparatory cleansings that Scaffolo Hutt had prescribed to begin his treatment.

A surly woodchuck had massaged Hermux with flax grease, covering him from head to toe with the nasty stuff. Then he had packed Hermux into a revolving drum filled with cedar and pine sawdust and set it to turning while wooden paddles pounded the mixture through Hermux's fur. After that he had vacuumed the sawdust out of Hermux's fur, wrapped Hermux in hot wet towels and left him lying on a bed beneath a heat lamp to swelter for twenty minutes.

Hermux stripped off one glove and examined his paw. The cactus pulp Paw Renew had congealed into sticky goop. He checked his watch again. It was time to shampoo it off.

He sat up and looked hopelessly at the pile of bottles, packets, tins and boxes on the coffee table, trying to remember the difference between an exfoliant and a defoliant. He picked up the purple bottle and read the label.

Ultra-nutri-Fur

total Restoration shampoo

All Natural!
Extra Silky!
Super Rich!

formulated exclusively for

the Last Resort
by
Tucka Mertslin

'I'm not even surprised,' he said. 'And what choice do I have? What choice have I had about anything?' he groaned. 'And I haven't had a single moment to look for Ms Perflinger.'

Clutching the purple bottle of Ultra-nutri-Fur, he trudged slowly towards the bathroom. 'Maybe a hot shower will perk me up.'

There was a sharp rap at the front door. Hermux retraced his footsteps to the living-room and answered the door.

It was the porter.

'Message for Mr Pulmix,' he said, extending a crisp grey envelope edged in navy blue. 'From Dr Mennus.'

Hermux took the envelope nervously.

'Thank you,' he said, fishing in his pocket for a tip.

The porter regarded the greasy quarter on Hermux's sticky, outstretched paw with a combination of disappointment and distaste. After an uncomfortably long moment, he picked it up carefully and wiped it off on his trouser leg before stowing it in his change purse.

'No reply expected,' he said gruffly and stalked away into the evening.

Hermux shut the door and tore open the envelope.

From the desk of
Hiril Mennus M.D.

My dear Mr Pulmix,

After reviewing your case with my senior staff, I believe it would be in your best interest to meet with me as soon as possible to discuss your treatment options . I will expect you at my office at 7.00 this evening.

Warm regards,

Mennus

Chapter 60
FACE TO FACE

It took Hermux three head-to-toe shampoos to finally get all the flax grease out of his fur. As much as he hated to admit it, Tucka's shampoo, which smelled just slightly of basil and pepper, was fresh and invigorating. As he towelled himself dry he noticed that his fur did seem both richer and silkier than he remembered it. And his silhouette in the steamy mirror looked noticeably more vigorous than usual, if he did say so himself. Hermux was hungry. He'd had nothing to eat all day but the small bowl of swede consommé that Nurse Tarmon had permitted him at lunch, but he felt energetic and alert.

'If I weren't here on a life-or-death mission, I could really learn to like this,' he said.

He dressed quickly and walked confidently across the leafy campus to the main building to face Dr Mennus himself. He felt quite like the determined little hero-in-the-making right up until the very moment he announced himself at the reception desk.

'Hermux,' he began. 'I beg your pardon, Torvin L. Pulmix to see Dr Mennus.'

206

'Do you have an appointment?' asked the hamster behind the desk.

'Yes,' stammered Hermux. 'For seven o'clock. I received a note.'

'Please be seated. I'll buzz Dr Mennus's office.'

She dialled a number, then turned away and spoke softly into the phone.

'He'll be with you in a moment,' she told Hermux.

Hermux sat down with relief. His knees suddenly felt very rubbery. He tried to appear calm while he prepared himself for his interview with Mennus. Was this a routine interview? Or was Mennus suspicious of something? What did he mean by treatment options?

'Stay alert!' he said to himself. 'Look for any clues to Linka's whereabouts. Figure out the layout of the laboratory. And above all don't forget you're Torvin L. Pulmix from Couver, Linoleum Dealer.'

The door to the laboratory opened and a grey rat in a starched white lab coat emerged.

'Dr Mennus will see you now,' he said. Hermux struggled clumsily to his feet. It was the same rat that he had tailed to Linka's house.

'This way,' said the rat and, without waiting for Hermux to follow, he turned and disappeared. Hermux barely got through the door before it slammed closed with the distinct click of a substantial lock. Hermux rushed after the rat, hoping that the door was only locked from one side.

Inside Hermux found a dimly lit hallway that sloped down towards the back of the building. Vague chemical smells hung in the air, which vibrated with the hum of equipment in use.

The rat stopped at a heavy oak door and knocked. A muffled voice inside responded. The rat opened the door and waved Hermux inside.

'Dr Mennus,' he said with a smirk. 'Mr Pulmix to see you.'

Hermux took a deep breath and stepped through the doorway.

'This is it!' he thought.

At first he could see nothing but a bright rectangle of light floating in semi-darkness. Then he realized that the rectangle was a window; that the window looked out over a large laboratory space; and that standing in front of the window was a solidly built figure. The figure turned towards him and spoke.

'Welcome to the Last Resort, Mr Pulmix,' said a voice that seemed to lower the already cool temperature of the room by several degrees.

Mennus turned from the window and pushed a button on the top of his desk. There was a mechanical whir as a heavy shade slowly descended over the window and closed off the view of the laboratory. The office was pitched into total darkness.

After an uncomfortably long moment, several small lamps flickered to life. But the room remained quite dark. As Hermux's eyes adjusted he could see that the walls were painted a rich, earthy brown. The same brown as the carpet. And nearly the same brown as the mass of twisted, tangled tree roots that rose up from the floor to form the base of an enormous desk behind which stood the doctor himself, staring intently at Hermux.

He was shorter than Hermux expected. And heavier,

considering that he owned a health spa and put people through the sort of torture that Hermux had just endured all day. But otherwise he looked much as he did in Pup's grainy photograph. He was dressed in the same immaculate, black smoking jacket. He wore the same dark glasses that completely concealed his eyes but did not disguise the elegant, gaunt lines of his face.

Mennus gave Hermux the impression of someone who never denied himself the pleasures of the table, but whose hunger was never satisfied.

'I trust your stay has been enjoyable so far?' said Mennus with a faint smile that revealed a row of very small but very sharp teeth.

'It's quite wonderful,' gushed Hermux. 'I've only been here a day, and I find myself feeling already extraordinarily fit.'

'Excellent,' said Mennus, coming out from behind his desk and standing very close to Hermux. 'Excellent. But there are other aspects of your health we must consider—longevity for example.'

Mennus laid his paw heavily on Hermux's shoulder and guided him towards the chair in front of his desk. 'I've been going over your evaluations, and I've noticed several disturbing trends.'

'You have?' asked Hermux anxiously.

'Small things only a trained eye would notice. But things that could shorten your life substantially. Why don't you have a seat?'

He gave Hermux a small shove, and Hermux sat down with a thump.

'My first question, Mr Pulmix, is how long have you been in the linoleum business?'

'Oh!' blurted Hermux. 'Years and years! Why, my father was in linoleum. And before that his uncle. I guess we've got linoleum in our blood.'

'My point precisely, Mr Pulmix,' said Mennus. He lifted what looked like a small brass spray gun from his desk and pointed it at Hermux. 'And how long is it that you've not been feeling quite like yourself?'

Hermux raised his hands protectively to ward off the poisonous spray.

But Mennus ignored him. He crossed to a long, low planter filled with clumps of fleshy, exotic-looking mushrooms. 'The trick with fungi is the right amount of light and sufficient moisture,' he explained as he pumped a fine mist from the sprayer. 'Like anything that feeds on rot. How long exactly have you been having these nervous fits?' He gestured pointedly at Hermux, who cowered in his chair.

'Fits?' asked Hermux.

'These feelings of imminent attack? Of persecution? Perhaps of being at the centre of some shadowy conspiracy?'

But Hermux didn't answer. He was studying a small machine on Mennus's desk. It was a gleaming maze of glass tubes and translucent chambers with little metal gears and drive shafts connected to rods and levers and valves and switches. It was altogether one of the most interesting mechanisms Hermux had ever seen.

Chapter 61
THE VISION THING

'I see you share my interest in mechanical devices,' said Mennus. His voice warmed with an unmistakable note of pride, and his interest in Hermux's health suddenly evaporated.

'Most interested!' answered Hermux with genuine enthusiasm. 'I tinker around a bit myself in my spare time. Nothing so elegant as this of course.'

'Then perhaps you might enjoy seeing a full-scale, working model,' beamed Mennus. 'Why don't we step down to my laboratory? It would give me great pleasure to demonstrate it to someone with a real appreciation for precision mechanics.'

Mennus ushered Hermux out of his office and into the hallway. They descended to the laboratory level, which was bustling with activity.

The white rat Hermux recognized from the limousine came towards them, wheeling a hospital stretcher with a sheet. Faint moans came from the crumpled figure on the stretcher.

'More problems, Mennus. The blow dry is still too hot.

And the stretch-and-firm is out of adjustment again. This one nearly croaked.'

Mennus silenced the rat with a sharp shake of his head and waved him out of the way.

'Naturally,' he explained to Hermux in a genial tone, 'there are always details to be ironed out. But once you see the big picture I think you'll agree that the extra trouble was worth it.'

He led Hermux on a complicated route among aisles of towering equipment until he reached a plywood construction partition with a door cut crudely into it. The sign on the door said:

EXTRA TOP SECRET
No Admittance
Without Explicit Permission from the Boss
THIS MEANS YOU!

Mennus unlocked the hefty padlock that secured the door and motioned for Hermux to follow him inside.

'And now,' he said proudly over his shoulder. 'One of the crowning achievements of an already distinguished career in science. I present the future of beauty–the U-Babe 2000 Automated-Beauty Centre.'

It was an impressive sight. Hermux gazed in honest admiration at the towering construction of gleaming glass and stainless steel. It was a gigantic version of the model, and seen in full scale it resembled an enclosed roller-coaster.

Mennus stepped up to the sleek control panel and threw a switch that brought the machine to life. A door opened, and with a sharp pneumatic hiss a clear Plexiglas capsule rolled into view. Mennus touched the control panel again and the top of the capsule sprang open. There was just enough room to lie down inside. 'I'll be remembered for many things,' he crowed exuberantly. 'But this may be my masterpiece! Hand me that hamster dummy!'

A young male hamster dressed in jeans and a sweatshirt lay on top of a bin of stuffed animals. Beneath it Hermux recognized several kinds of mice and rats, an otter, a mink, a gopher, a mole—all of them fully dressed and very lifelike in scale and appearance. Hermux lifted the hamster and carried it to Mennus. It was quite heavy, and the fur on its head felt quite genuine. Hermux had an uncomfortable feeling that it might actually be genuine.

He handed the hamster over to Mennus with a shiver. Mennus dropped the hamster unceremoniously into the capsule and pressed the large red button on the control panel. The top of the capsule dropped shut with a bang and an explosive burst of air shoved the capsule violently into the large clear tube that ran diagonally up the outside of the machine.

As the capsule rose through the tube it began to spin faster and faster until it appeared to Hermux as though the dummy's clothes were being thrown from its body by centrifugal force.

'Now you see where value-added thinking comes into play,' Mennus told him.

There was a sharp hiss and a clang, and the hamster's clothes shot out of the capsule and were sucked into a network of clear tubing that carried them away into the interior of the machine.

'In addition to comprehensive, long-term beautification,' Mennus explained, 'the U-Babe 2000 cleans and presses the

213

user's clothes and returns them to him or her at the end of the treatment. But now for the truly sophisticated functions of the machine …'

He called Hermux's attention to the lighted display screen that showed icons of animal types. He clicked on the hamster icon, and a new screen appeared with a series of hamster silhouettes that ranged from short to tall, from thin to fat, and from anaemic to robust.

'I would say that our victim, I mean our subject, is of medium height, more than a bit overweight, and of a slightly less than vigorous build.' He clicked each of the icons in turn. 'And now for the Magic of Mennus. Our starting point is what our subject is, but our finishing point is what our subject would like to be. And the answers are obvious. Tall rather than short. Thin rather than fat. But not too thin, of course, as the subject is not female. And muscular.'

As he spoke he continued clicking icons at a dizzying speed.

The screen went blank for a moment. Then messages appeared:

```
Processing your request.

Are you certain?  Yes. No.
```

Mennus clicked *Yes* without any hesitation. Hermux heard the low sound of a large motor beginning to turn and slowly building up to speed.

'Come with me,' said Mennus and began to ascend a narrow winding staircase that led up into the machine. 'I think

I can assure you that you will be astonished at what you're about to see.'

Hermux had to strain to hear Mennus's voice above the increasing roar of the machine's motors.

They were almost at the top when Mennus stopped and pointed triumphantly below them. The Plexiglas capsule had come to a stop in a sealed chamber beneath the catwalk they were standing on. The capsule opened and two mechanical arms extended towards the hamster dummy. It was lifted into the air and carried slowly towards what looked to Hermux like an electric sewing-machine. The mechanical arms began to revolve the dummy and the sewing-machine began to stitch. As he watched in complete amazement the shape of the dummy began to change.

'I have completely automated my full-body-sculpt process. I can totally reshape any body to any standard of beauty using my patented surgical stitching technique.'

'It looks like a cross between a rotisserie and a sewing-machine,' said Hermux without thinking.

'And so it is, my observant little mouse, but I have had each of them modified to my rigorous and secret specifications.'

Below them the robot arms ran the hamster back and forth through the sewing-machine, turning, tilting, raising and lowering it in precise increments. Then the sewing-machine stopped abruptly. A third robot arm bearing a pair of scissors appeared and began methodically to snip the loose ends of the sutures.

'Less than two minutes,' boasted Mennus, tapping his watch for Hermux to see. 'A procedure like that would take me more than eight hours to perform manually. Instead I have done it simply, quickly, and automatically. So quickly in fact that many subjects will feel only minimal pain.'

The scissors finished snipping.

Hermux gaped in astonishment. What had been an ordinary, slightly pudgy hamster was now a narrow-waisted, broad-shouldered party animal. The mechanical arms returned the hamster to its capsule, and with a pneumatic burst of air the capsule dropped into a chute and disappeared from view.

'From here it's more routine,' said Mennus, satisfied with the impact of his demonstration. 'Condition, wash, trim, brush and blow dry. Plus colour of course. What do you think of it?'

'It's remarkable,' said Hermux. And he meant it.

'Naturally the concept is brilliant,' Mennus continued as he led the way back down the stairs. 'It's mine after all. But in this case I think my execution is even more impeccable than usual. The quality of the surgery is in many cases very nearly comparable to what I would do myself by hand. And think of the reduction in costs! A full body makeover will only be a tiny fraction of what it would cost you in a clinic. And of course, there is the convenience factor. Picture it, Pulmix, thousands of these machines in operation. One in every shopping centre in the country. It won't even be necessary to have an appointment. Think of the boost in national beauty averages! Think of the profit margins. No more overpaid nursing staff. No expensive real estate. No overhead at all really. Just simple maintenance. And I've managed to automate most of that. It's foolproof.'

Moments after they reached the control panel again, the machine gave a noisy belch and the hamster, fully dressed, shampooed and brushed, popped out in its shiny, clear capsule.

Mennus dragged it out and held it up for Hermux's admiration. Hermux couldn't help noticing the obsessive quality of Mennus's attention to detail. The hamster's clothes had also been altered to fit its new body. And they fitted perfectly.

On closer examination, however, it did seem to Hermux that the hamster's left arm was bent into a rather unnatural angle.

'What happens if someone makes a mistake?' inquired Hermux.

'What do you mean by mistake?'

'Well, what if someone chooses the wrong body type to start with or the wrong one to end up with? What if someone with a long tail for example mistakenly clicks on a short-tailed species?'

'That would be unfortunate, as you can imagine,' admitted Mennus as he tossed the hamster back on to the bin of dummies. 'However, such an event seems highly unlikely. Our instruction manual explains the U-Babe's operations very carefully.'

The white rat appeared at the door and motioned for Mennus's attention.

'Mennus, we've got a bit of a problem with our special guest,' he said. 'It needs your attention. A.S.A.P. '

Chapter 62
LOUNGE LIZARD

Mennus frowned at the interruption. He thought for a moment. Then he flipped the off switch on the U-Babe 2000 and told Hermux to follow him.

Mennus moved surprisingly quickly, and Hermux scampered to keep up.

'You will wait in here,' Mennus commanded, stopping and pushing Hermux towards a door marked Employee Lounge. 'Make yourself comfortable. This shouldn't take long.'

Then he scuttled off towards an unmarked door barely visible in the shadows at the back of the lab. The white rat remained behind, watching Hermux curiously and stroking his whiskers with a peculiar, nervous gesture.

'I guess I'll go inside and sit down,' Hermux told him.

'Why not?' said the rat indifferently.

Hermux opened the door and peered inside. The Employee Lounge didn't look comfortable. But it was more appealing to Hermux than standing alone in the lab with an odd rat staring at him.

The door swung closed behind him. The lounge was a

small sparsely furnished room. It was dark and stuffy and had an odd odour that was far from pleasant. There was a refrigerator, a table, several folding chairs, and a bed pushed up against the outside wall. High over the bed was a small window.

Hermux looked hard at the window. Barely visible through the smudged glass was the outline of a shrub. The window was at ground level outside. It was big enough for Hermux to crawl through. And Hermux thought that if he put a chair on the bed and stood on it and reached his very furthest, he might reach the top of the window and be able to unlock it.

He listened carefully at the door. No one was coming. He grabbed the nearest chair and set it firmly on the mattress of the bed. It was a very springy, soft mattress, and the chair rocked and sagged as he clambered up on it. But he clung to the wall and managed to stay upright, scrabbling his claws to reach the windowsill and pulling himself up with a strength that surprised even him. He grasped the lock in one paw and twisted hard. It was stuck. He tried again. This time he threw his whole weight into it. The chair tipped wildly and slipped out from beneath him. Hermux dropped with a bang, still holding on to the lock, and nearly wrenched his arm from its socket. The lock snapped open, and Hermux fell like a stone. He bounced off the mattress and landed face down on the table. He staggered back to the bed, grabbed the chair, carried it to the table and collapsed dizzily on to it just as Mennus threw open the door, and announced with obvious satisfaction, 'I think that's taken care of.'

Hermux smiled up at him feebly, wheezing for breath.

'Tomorrow, Mr Pulmix, I think we'll have to step up your aerobic conditioning. We've hardly moved at all this evening, and you're completely winded.'

Chapter 63
PHONE HOME

When he stepped back inside the lobby, Hermux was elated by what he had done and relieved that he had survived his first encounter with Dr Mennus without fainting. He looked at his watch. It was nearly nine o'clock. He should call Pup.

The pay phones were directly across the lobby from the reception desk. The receptionist gave Hermux a bored look and went back to reading her paperback. Hermux sauntered around the fountain, slowly pretending to admire it. Then when he was sure he was out of sight, he ducked into a phone booth and quietly slid its door closed.

He got out his wallet and found the slip of paper with Pup's phone number written on it. He dropped a quarter into the phone and dialled.

Pup answered on the first ring.

'Schoonagliffen here!'

'Pup? It's Hermux.'

'Tantamoq! What's up? Have you found her?'

'No. But I've got a lead. I think she's being held in Mennus's private laboratory. I met him tonight, and I managed to unlock a window in the employee lounge right off the lab. Once it's quiet, I'll let myself back in and check things out.'

'Be careful, Tantamoq! The more I know about this character the less I like him. Do you think he suspects anything?'

'No. As far as he knows, I'm just a nervous linoleum dealer from Couver with an interest in machinery. Any word on Dandiffer?'

'I've traced him as far as the hospital in Teulabonari. It looks like he's left there and is heading back here to Pinchester.'

'I only hope I'm in time to save Ms Perflinger, Pup! Now that I've seen what Mennus is capable of, I'm even more worried about her. He is a genuine nutcase.'

'Well, do what you can. I'll expect a call from you first thing in the morning. If I don't hear from you, I'll go to the police with what we've got!'

Chapter 64
NIGHT JOURNEY

Shortly after midnight the door of the Ivy Bungalow opened without a sound, and a small dark figure slipped out into the night. Hermux stepped off the porch and stopped to get his bearings. He buttoned his old jacket against the chill fog and sniffed the air carefully.

He wasn't really sure what a snake smelled like. He had only seen them in photographs. But he imagined that they smelled leathery and bitter. There was nothing strange in the air except a hint of honeysuckle, so he crept forward cautiously, feeling his way along the walk that led to the main building. When he thought he was halfway there, he left the walk and cut across the lawn in what he hoped was a direct line towards the laboratory. Before long he saw the indistinct glow of the lights and found himself creeping along a low hedge at the base of the building.

He came to a bank of large windows that he assumed was the main lab. He crawled into the hedge below the windows and listened. Inside he could hear the hum of machinery and occasional voices. Hermux worked his way along the base of the wall in the direction of the lounge. A trail of some sort had been worn into the hedge, and Hermux made good progress.

Soon he was peering through the window into the empty lounge. He settled down patiently to wait. And he didn't have to wait very long. The sound of the lab machinery began to wind down. One by one the lights in the lab windows were extinguished. Finally someone opened the door to the lounge and switched off the light. A deep silence fell over the Last Resort.

Hermux readied himself, his tail twitching in anticipation. He inserted the tips of his front claws into the top edge of the window casing and pulled it gently towards him. It moved slightly. He pulled harder. It gave suddenly and fell open with a shrill squeak.

Hermux's heart pounded so furiously that he thought he could hear the blood coursing through his ears. Then he realized in horror that it wasn't his ears he was hearing. It was the sound of something sliding over dry leaves. Something was slithering along the ground next to the building. And it was moving very fast. An unfamiliar sharp smell rose in the night air.

In one motion Hermux leapt through the window and pulled it closed behind him. As he fell through the air, he heard something strike hard against the glass. Then he hit the bed.

Chapter 65
STRAPPED FOR TIME

Hermux landed awkwardly on his side. The fall knocked the wind out of him, and he twisted his ankle. He gasped for breath and struggled to sit up. The window above him rattled noisily from the impact of something hitting it again. Hermux cringed and clambered down from the bed. He tested his ankle. It was sore. But he could walk. He inched his way across the floor in the darkness, skirting the table and chairs, and slid his paw along the wall until he found the doorframe. He put his ear against the door and listened. All he could hear was his own uneven breathing.

He grasped the doorknob and turned it cautiously.

It wouldn't move. He turned harder. It was frozen in place. Then to his shocked amazement it came alive in his hand–twisting of its own accord. The door was yanked open, the room was flooded with light, and Hermux found himself face to face with Dr Mennus.

'I hope we haven't kept you waiting, Mr Pulmix,' said Mennus sarcastically. 'I know that I hate to be kept waiting. And what is it here, I wonder, that has so captivated your curiosity? Boys! Mr Pulmix must be exhausted after his trip. I think he should lie down.'

Two lab rats pushed their way past Mennus into the lounge. Hermux raised his arms to resist, but he was no match for the tall, rangy rats. They wrestled him to his back on the bed. Then they strapped him down tightly with thick leather straps. Mennus himself buckled the straps in place and locked them.

'It's not that I no longer trust you, Mr Pulmix,' he explained slyly as he pocketed the key. 'But in your deteriorating nervous condition, I would feel responsible if you were to, let's say, hurt yourself.'

'How long do you think you can hold me here before I'm missed?'

'Well, that depends on how long it is before the folks in Couver miss you. Doesn't it?' Mennus responded with a meaningful smile.

'Of course,' he continued, 'it might not be necessary to hold you at all. Especially if you decide to confide in me. I am, after all, your doctor. You can tell me everything. And if you can explain to my satisfaction who you really are, why you're really here, and what you're looking for, I may be able to prescribe the proper treatment for you. Until then I think we'll have to rely on a straightforward series of electro-shocks to settle your nerves. I've scheduled them to begin first thing tomorrow morning. That will give you the rest of the night to think it over, Mr Pulmix. Pleasant dreams until then.'

Mennus checked each of the straps once again. Then he and the rats left, turning out the lights and closing the door behind them.

Chapter 66
A HISS IN THE DARK

Hermux struggled to free himself, but he was pinned tight beneath the straps. All he could move were his head and his feet. He tried to rock the bed back and forth, thinking that maybe he could knock it over. But it wouldn't budge.

He gave up and considered his situation. Even to a beginner at adventure, it didn't look good.

In the morning when Pup didn't hear from him, he would go to the police. And the police might do something. But then again they might not. And even if the police did come to the Last Resort, what would they find?

What condition would he be in after Mennus began the shock treatments?

Or would Mennus file charges against him as a burglar who had been caught red-handed and had checked into the clinic under an assumed name?

'What a fool I've been,' he said ruefully to the empty lounge. 'Hermux Tantamoq, Watchmaker and Professional Blunderer. I walked right into a trap.'

There was a scrabbling tap at the window. And another.

227

Then a faint, scratching sound. Hermux stared up in terror as the window creaked and began to open.

Next he expected the head of a snake to poke through. And then he knew he would be swallowed whole—just as he had seen once in a magazine.

Instead, he heard a loud whisper.

'Tantamoq! Are you there?'

It was Pup.

Chapter 67
REINFORCEMENTS

'I'm right here, Pup,' said Hermux. 'I was caught.'

The beam of a tiny flashlight swept the room and stopped at Hermux on the bed.

'Good show, old mouse!' exclaimed Pup at the sight of the straps. 'Looks like you put up quite a fight!'

He squeezed halfway through the window and lowered himself down the wall as far as he could. He dropped heavily on to the bed and landed with one foot on Hermux's stomach.

'Ow!' grunted Hermux.

'Sorry, old mouse,' apologized Pup. 'It was further than I expected.'

He jumped down and began to work on the straps.

'I got worried after you called, thinking about you being all alone. I said to myself, 'Pup, get yourself out there and see what you and Tantamoq can do together. This may be too big a job for one mouse.' And it looks like I was right. I left my scooter just outside the gate and walked in. I tried every window along this wall. Say! These straps are locked! Who's got the key?'

'Mennus has it. What can we do?'

'Let me think. Let me think. Where's Mennus?'

'He probably went back to his office. I think he works very late.'

'Are there any tools in the lab? Is there anything I could use to cut the straps?'

'I don't know. I didn't get to look around much, but there are storage cabinets all along the walls beneath the windows.'

'Stay here, then,' whispered Pup. 'Sorry! Of course you'll stay here. I'll go look for something and come back for you. Where's Perflinger?'

'There's a door at the very back of the lab. I think she's in there. Be careful, Pup. Mennus is very cagey.'

'Don't worry. I sneak around in places all the time.'

He opened the door a crack and slipped through, closing it behind him without a sound.

Hermux waited nervously. Ten minutes passed. And Pup didn't return. Then there was a loud crash in the lab. Hermux strained his head towards the door. Someone shouted and lights came on out in the lab.

There were sounds of a struggle. And then silence.

Moments later the door opened, and the two lab rats pushed Pup roughly into the room.

Pup met Hermux's eyes and shrugged sadly. He said nothing.

'Get some rope!' said the bigger of the two rats. 'I'll watch him.'

The smaller rat returned with a coil of rope, and the two of them forced Pup into a chair. Then they bound him methodically, tying his hands and ankles tightly.

When they were done the bigger rat gave Pup a hard kick to test the knots.

'This will hold,' he said satisfied. 'Now we'd better tell Mennus what's up.'

Chapter 68
ROPE TRICK

As soon as the rats were gone, Pup began to squirm about in his chair.

'Sorry, Tantamoq,' he said, twisting his legs from side to side and hunching down low. 'The place is booby-trapped. I set one off, and they pounced on me. Those rats are rough customers. I think they hurt my shoulder.'

'Looks like we're sunk, Pup. I'm sorry I got you mixed up in this.'

'Nonsense,' said Pup taking a deep breath. 'It's been grand so far. And I'm making progress here.'

He gave a wild jerk with his whole body, and the rope came loose and fell away from him into a loose pile on the floor.

Hermux stared in amazement.

'Surprising, isn't it? I wrote an article last year on circuses, carnivals and magic shows. Picked up a few useful tricks.'

Then Pup looked at Hermux seriously.

'But we're right back where we started,' he said. 'Any suggestions?'

Hermux thought hard.

'Look, Pup. You've got to get out of here! Go back to town and go to the police.'

'Okay. But what am I going to tell them?'

'Tell them the whole story. From the beginning.'

'But we still don't have any proof!'

'Yes, we do, Pup! I've got Dandiffer's formula. Show them that.'

Pup leaned forward expectantly.

'Where is it?'

'It's in my apartment. My keys are in my pocket. It's the double-sided brass key. There's a cage on a stand in my study. The formula is hidden under the newspaper on the bottom.'

'All right. Maybe that will do it,' said Pup. He retrieved the keys from Hermux's pocket.

'There's one more thing, Pup. Dandiffer sent a chemical catalyst of some sort. It's in the little tin by the cage. Show them that.'

'Perfect!' said Pup with a broad smile.

There were noises in the lab—voices and sounds of someone coming.

'Go on, Pup! I'll be okay!'

But Pup didn't move. He seemed frozen, lost in thought. There were voices and footsteps just outside the door.

'Run for it, Pup! Go out the window! I'll be all right. Really!'

'I've no doubt about that, my little friend,' said Pup. He sounded quite strange to Hermux.

But it was too late for Pup to run. The door opened, and the two rats rushed in. This time they had guns.

Chapter 69
WHO'S WHO

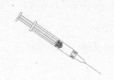

'Poor Pup!' said Hermux pitifully. 'What a mess I've got you in.'

'Well, technically,' said Pup, 'I'm afraid it is I who have got you into the mess. Of course, if you had minded your own business from the start you wouldn't be in a mess at all. Disappointing, isn't it?'

Then Pup reached up and tugged at his big front teeth. And to Hermux's everlasting horror Pup's cheerful, disarming smile came away in his hand, revealing a row of smallish, pointed teeth.

Pup put two fingers into his mouth and pulled out two rubber pouches. His plump, cheerful cheeks collapsed into gaunt creases.

Then he unbuttoned his dapper jacket, unsnapped his waistcoat, and let out a deep sigh of relief.

'You have no idea how uncomfortable that is!'

Pup's whole body sagged forward, revealing a pudgy little paunch. He removed a pair of dark glasses from his waistcoat pocket and fitted them to his face. Snappy, energetic Pup

Schoonagliffen was gone. And standing in his place was the treacherous and sinister Hiril Mennus, M.D.

'Here!' he snapped at the smaller white rat. 'This is the key to the little one's apartment. The formula is in the tray of the ladybird's cage. The catalyst is in the food tin. Get them and get back here immediately.'

Mennus turned to the bigger rat. 'Well played,' he said and then kicked him viciously in the shin. 'But the kick was overdone, you moron!'

Hermux stared at Mennus. Finally he spoke.

'You've manipulated me all along!' he sputtered furiously. 'You lured me here! You set me up! You betrayed me!'

'You betrayed yourself, you meddling little fool. Who asked you to get involved anyway? Spying on people! Breaking into their houses! Sneaking around behind their backs! Opening their mail! If you had given me the formula like I asked, you'd still be living your pointless little watchmaker's life. And you'd never have known the difference.'

'But Ms Perflinger!' exploded Hermux.

'Ms Perflinger!' hissed Mennus threateningly. 'Another stubborn meddler. I quite see the attraction, you know. Two interfering imbeciles poking their noses where they don't belong. If Perflinger had stayed out of Teulabonari to begin with, she'd still be dashing about the globe like the do-good lunatic that she is. And my factories would already be humming away. Cranking out eternal youth for the masses. And millions for me.'

'You villain!' snarled Hermux. 'You double-crossing mole!'

'Pike, get me my hypodermic,' Mennus told the bigger rat.

'The excitement has gotten Mr Tantamoq overwrought. I think he's ready for a long, quiet rest!'

Chapter 70
DEADLY MACHINATIONS

Hermux had no idea how long he had been unconscious. He vaguely heard voices and felt himself being moved, but his body seemed miles away. When Pike and the other lab rat lifted him from the bed and dropped him on the stretcher, he landed with a thud.

'This one's heavier than he looks!' whined the smaller one.

'Is he awake?' asked the bigger one.

'No way! That shot Mennus gave him would stun a beaver. He's lucky to be breathing.'

'Or not so lucky!'

They laughed wickedly.

'Or not so lucky!' they chanted together as they pushed the stretcher out of the lounge and into the lab.

Hermux tried to open his eyes, but the blinding light caused his head to pound wildly. He tried to sit up, but all he could do was roll his head to the side. The motion of the stretcher made him feel queasy. He was afraid that he was going to be sick. But suddenly he was hoisted up in the air by his hands and feet and dropped roughly on a hard wooden platform.

'Strap him down!' said the smaller rat.

Hermux felt the first strap tighten across his ankles. Then one above his knees. Then another across his stomach that clamped his paws at his sides. But before they could tighten it, Hermux had just enough energy to take the deepest breath he could. He struggled to hold his breath while they struggled to buckle the strap.

'A regular little porker!' snickered the smaller rat. 'Maybe we should run him through the U-Babe here before we get started.'

'I think this treatment will take the weight off him!'

'Ssssssh! Here comes Mennus!'

'All right, boys! Finish up and get the girl!' Mennus instructed them tersely. 'Intermission is nearly over! It's time to raise the curtain on the last act.'

The rats disappeared with the stretcher.

Mennus walked to the water cooler and came back with a glass of water. He stood over Hermux and studied him for a moment. Then he tossed the water in the groggy mouse's face.

'Rise and shine, Tantamoq! I don't want you to miss a moment of this.'

Hermux sputtered and opened his eyes.

'You see I've prepared something very special for you in return for the formula and the catalyst. They were both delivered to me safely just now,' said Mennus grandly. 'It's a sort of going away present.'

While Mennus talked Hermux tried to get his bearings. They had moved him to the top secret work area. Behind

Mennus he could see the outlines of the U-Babe 2000. He couldn't see any means of escape.

Mennus droned on, 'And knowing how you love well-made machinery, being a watchmaker and all that, I knew you'd want a little technical background before we set things in motion. And then I've really got to get to work in the lab. So much to do. So little time!'

The rats returned with the stretcher. And there was someone on it. Someone familiar. Turning his head as far as he could, Hermux could see that it was Ms Perflinger.

She was bound hand and foot, and her mouth was covered by a wide strip of adhesive tape. She looked thin and exhausted. But when they lifted her off the stretcher she struggled to get free. Her eyes blazed with anger and determination.

'Yes, Tantamoq. Ms Perflinger at last!'

They dumped Ms Perflinger unceremoniously on the platform next to Hermux.

'How charming to see you reunited,' gloated Mennus. 'It's a pity your acquaintance is doomed to be so brief. Now boys, bring in my little project.'

'I hope they haven't hurt you, Ms Perflinger!' said Hermux earnestly.

Ms Perflinger looked at Hermux hopefully and then Mennus. She narrowed her eyes in distaste.

'Tut! Tut!' interrupted Mennus. 'Time for that later. Not much time of course. But some ...'

The rats rolled in a tall apparatus that looked a lot like a grandfather clock mechanism that had been removed from its case.

'I've never liked this thing,' confided Mennus, positioning it next to Hermux and locking the wheels. 'Family heirloom and all that. But it's finally serving a purpose.'

He extended a cable from a pulley at the top of the clock, ran it over Hermux's head, and hooked it to a heavy metal bar that ran around the wooden platform.

'What the devil is he up to now?' wondered Hermux, squirming to get a better view. Then Mennus picked up a sort of leather harness, which he fitted tightly around Hermux's chest. Then he pulled a short wire from the clock mechanism and snapped it to the harness.

As Hermux took his next breath the wire from the harness pulled against the clock. There was a ratcheting sound. The gears of the clock advanced a single notch. The cable over Hermux's head tightened slightly.

'Now this is what I mean when I say 100% mouse-powered technology,' said Mennus. He removed a watchmaker's wrench from a small toolbox and made some adjustments in the harness and the cable. 'Incidentally, Tantamoq, I must compliment you on your choice of tools. These are really first rate!'

'Those are my grandfather's tools!' blurted Hermux. 'How dare you?'

'I know it was naughty,' said Mennus. 'But they were right there in your hall cupboard. And it didn't seem like you were using them. So Pike brought them back with the formula. And look, they're just perfect for what we're doing. I'll leave them right here.'

'Now, are you both comfy?' Mennus asked. 'It won't do for you to be uncomfortable. You'll just rush things and spoil the fun! You see the genius of the thing is that you do the work yourself. I'm merely here to set things in motion. And of course, when the time comes, to say good-bye.

'Now as you can see,' Mennus pointed out, 'the harness is connected to the wire. The wire is connected to the clock. The clock is connected to the cable. And the cable is connected to ...'

Mennus paused and looked at Hermux wonderingly. 'Ah! That's the question isn't it? What is the cable connected to? Any guesses? Surely, Tantamoq! You should have guessed it by now!'

Hermux's eyes followed the cable from the clock to the metal bar. He twisted his head to trace the bar around the edge of the platform to its origin in a big coiled spring just behind Ms Perflinger's back. There was something vaguely familiar about it all. But from his angle it was hard to see how it all fitted together. Hermux looked up at Mennus as he leaned over in eager anticipation. He watched the glint of Mennus's dark glasses. And then suddenly he saw it.

'Even you can't be that bad!' Hermux groaned.

'Oh, but I can!' chuckled Mennus. 'I can! And I am!'

Hermux could see himself and Ms Perflinger clearly reflected in the black mirrors of Mennus's glasses. He could see how all the parts fitted together. He could see the outlines of the wooden platform. He could see that the metal bar surrounded only half of the platform. And that it was actually part of the coiled spring. And then it all snapped into place. And he could see that he and Ms Perflinger were strapped inside a large mousetrap.

He took a deep breath, felt the movement of the harness,

heard the turning of the clock, and watched in disbelief as the bar rose slightly.

'You're mad, Mennus. You'll never get away with this!'

'Oh, but I will, Tantamoq!' said Mennus. 'I will. I always do! Now, before I excuse myself and get to work on that formula, I'll explain a few of the machine's fine points. As you can see, you're in complete control of its operation. You may breathe as slowly or as quickly as you wish. Take your time, or move things along according to your preferences. Now here's my favourite touch and one I know you'll appreciate. It took me quite a while to work it out. But I've geared the platform to slide forward as you raise the bar here. That way, once you've set the trap, as they say, you'll be in a position to get the full therapeutic benefit of its operation. Now I've really got to run. And besides, I'm sure the two of you have a lot to talk about.'

Chapter 71
ROOM TO WIGGLE

They lay side by side in a state of shock listening to the creak of Mennus's deadly machine. It was some time before Hermux felt able to turn to Ms Perflinger.

'I'm so terribly sorry!' he told her. 'Mennus is a monster, and the worst of it is that I thought he was my friend. I'm afraid I've blundered right along with his plans every step of the way. I feel like a terrible fool.'

Ms Perflinger gazed at him with liquid brown eyes. As bad as things looked, she didn't seem to blame Hermux for her predicament. And once he thought it through, he didn't either. He had tried his best. And if the situation was over his head, perhaps it was because he had never before encountered a villain as heartless as Mennus. Someone who could pretend to be a friend while all along they were luring you into an elaborate trap. Just thinking about it made Hermux madder than he had ever been.

Ms Perflinger began to struggle against the ropes that held her. And Hermux decided that he wasn't ready to accept defeat just yet.

'I'm going to try to get my hands loose,' he explained to Ms Perflinger.

He took a deep breath in and let it out as far as he could, pushing his chest down and trying to pull his right arm free of the strap that held it at his side. He was able to move his arm slightly. He breathed in again and out, willing himself to feel thinner. He pulled hard, and his arm slipped. One more breath, and it was free.

He tried to loosen his left arm. But its circulation had been cut off. It had fallen asleep, and he couldn't move it. He tried to unbuckle the straps, but they were locked. He tried to unfasten the harness from the clock, but he couldn't manage with a single paw. He saw that the trap had risen nearly half way. He felt himself beginning to panic. And he knew that he needed more time.

He felt through his jacket pocket. But there was nothing there but a few coins and what felt like the broken remains of a crisp.

'But I haven't had a crisp in months,' he thought. Then he remembered standing in Ms Perflinger's house nibbling a moon plant leaf and putting the rest of it in his jacket pocket. He was sure of it. It was the moon plant. He licked his paw and with wet fingers he began to retrieve the fragments of the moon plant. He ate every single crumb, then played absent-mindedly with the coins as he tried to think. If he could just reach his grandfather's toolbox maybe he could get his snips and cut through the straps. If he could just stop time until the numbness in his left arm went away.

That was it. Hermux would try to stop time, just as Nock Noddem had. And he would use a nickel to do it.

244

Hermux took a nickel from his pocket and held it tightly between the tips of two fingers. He took a deep breath in, and as he reached towards the clock mechanism he let it out and turned his body as far as he could to the side. He strained towards the clock. His fingers grazed the large drive gear. His arm shook with the effort. And the nickel fell with a clatter to the floor.

Hermux glanced over at Ms Peflinger. She nodded her head encouragingly. He tried again with his last nickel. He breathed in. He breathed out. He turned, stretched, reached, and finally managed to lodge the nickel in the teeth of the gear. The clock made a grinding sound and lurched to a stop. The bar of the mousetrap hung motionless in space nearly three quarters of the way to the top.

Hermux grasped the edge of the mousetrap and pulled himself over as far as he could. He could make out the outlines of his grandfather's toolbox in the shadows. If he could free both arms he might be able to reach it. He rubbed his left arm vigorously. He could feel the blood returning. His arm tingled. It itched. It throbbed. He wiggled his fingers, and he began to work it free.

Chapter 72

IMPORTANT NEWSBREAK

Stretching to his utmost, Hermux managed to snag the handle on the toolbox and pull it towards him on the floor. But before he could open it, Mennus's voice rang out through the lab, 'Tantamoq!'

There was a rush of footsteps.

'Tantamoq! I've got it!' shouted Mennus. 'I've got the formula for eternal youth!'

Mennus rushed in just as Hermux struggled back into place and flattened his arms at his sides.

'Oh thank goodness!' he gushed. 'You're still here! I mean, of course you're still here, but you're still HERE. That's what's important!'

Hermux wondered for a brief moment if Mennus had changed his mind.

'Before you go, I wanted to thank you for helping with the formula,' Mennus went on. Triumphantly he raised a glass flask half-filled with a dark liquid. 'I really couldn't have done it without you. Both of you really! And to show my appreciation I've written a little memorial for you. It's a special good-bye from Pup. I just wanted to get your comments, if any, while you were still available.

'It's only a first draft,' he told them. 'So there may be some rough spots. But here goes …' As he began to read the typewritten article, Mennus's voice took on the familiar, eager tone of Pup Schoonagliffen.

Love Goes Wrong

Local Watchmaker Slays Adventuress and Self in Bizarre Suicide Machine

—Two longtime Pinchester residents were killed instantly last night in what police are calling a murder/suicide.

Hermux Tantamoq allegedly abducted aviatrix Linka Perflinger from her bungalow at the ultra-posh health spa the Last Resort. Then he killed both her and himself using an elaborate apparatus that he had secretly constructed on the premises.

Reached by telephone this morning, medical director Dr Hiril Mennus provided details of the horrific crime.

'Apparently Tantamoq had been stalking Ms Perflinger for some time,' said Mennus. 'She was terrified of him. She told me that he had harassed her verbally and broken into her home. He had even sent her an obscene photograph of himself. The police found it when they searched her home this morning. She tried to escape him, but he traced her here to the Last Resort. He checked in the day before yesterday under an assumed name and wearing a disguise. He was caught breaking into one of our laboratories. Unfortunately he escaped and hid himself in an unused section of our laboratory. He was apparently able to assemble his horrific machine without being detected.'

A police spokeswoman confirmed that a chest of Tantamoq's watchmaking tools was found at the scene of the crime, but she would not elaborate on the nature of the apparatus. An unconfirmed rumour suggests that Tantamoq used his watchmaking skills to create an automated mousetrap, which he then turned against himself and his victim.

As the gruesome details of the tragedy emerge, residents of Pinchester ask themselves what could have been done to prevent it.

Downtown Postlady Lista Blenwipple knew Tantamoq for years. 'I've worried about Mr Tantamoq all spring. He was obsessed by Ms Perflinger. He told me recently that if he couldn't have her, no one could.'

'I never said that!' interrupted Hermux angrily.

'I know,' admitted Mennus. 'But don't you wish you had? It's so romantic!'

'And you took that photograph! It was Nurse Tarmon! She told me it was for your records!'

'And so it was! And now you see why it's so important for me to keep good records.'

Mennus peered anxiously at Hermux and Linka. 'Well? What do you think of it overall?' he asked hopefully. 'Is the tone right? Be honest.'

'I think that you're completely insane,' said Hermux in a low, level voice. 'You need help. Pup? Listen to me. I know you're not all bad. You've got to let us go. We'll help you.'

'You'll help me? You insignificant little blunderer! You'll help me? The discoverer of the formula for eternal youth? The hero of the entire affluent world? I don't think so!' he snapped. 'Say? What's taking this thing so long anyway? It's not even moving!' he said angrily.

Mennus stooped by the machine and peered inside. 'What's this?' he said, pulling the nickel from the gears. The machine jerked into motion again.

'What's going on here?'

His eyes darted wildly around the lab. 'Who's here?'

He grabbed up the flask of youth formula.

'I'll take that!' said a gravelly voice from the doorway. 'I paid for it. It's mine. And it's overdue!'

It was Tucka Mertslin. She was dressed in a black Lurex catsuit. With furry kit-kat ears and a long slinky tail. She had a silver pistol levelled at Mennus.

'Thank goodness!' exclaimed Hermux. 'Tucka! Stop the machine before we're killed!'

Tucka gave him a withering look. She had no interest in the machine or Hermux.

'How did you get in here?' demanded Mennus.

'I own the place, you imbecile. I have keys! Now give me the formula and the flask!'

'This, you mean?' asked Mennus, removing a folded sheet of paper from his lab coat. As he held it up a cigarette lighter appeared in his other hand. And before Tucka could move, the formula was in flames.

Chapter 73
A STITCH IN TIME

Mennus dropped the burning formula, and Tucka lunged for it. She stamped the flames wildly with her stiletto heels, quickly extinguishing the flames but unfortunately shredding the formula into tiny pieces.

She turned on Mennus in a fury. 'Give me the flask,' she growled and motioned with the gun.

'Make me!' he taunted. And with a single swift motion he raised the flask to his lips.

'Don't do that!' cautioned Hermux.

But it was too late. Mennus had drunk it completely.

He threw off his dark glasses, and there was a wild look in his eyes. He knocked the gun from Tucka's hand.

'Now youth is mine!' he chortled. 'It's all mine! The formula's right up here!' he said, pointing at his head. 'And there's nothing you can do about it! I'm getting out of here! Starting fresh in a new place. With no Tucka Mertslin. Thanks again, Ms Perflinger! And thanks in advance for the use of your aeroplane!'

He started towards the door. And then a huge spasm

shook his body from head to toe. His eyes twitched. His head jerked from side to side.

Hermux stared at him in wonder.

Then Mennus began to shrink. For a moment he looked like Pup Schoonagliffen again. Trim and energetic. Then he looked like a young Pup Schoonagliffen. Then a very young Pup. He shrank faster and faster. The flask dropped from his hand and broke into pieces on the floor. From the spot where Mennus had stood, a baby mole stared up at them helplessly. He raised his arms and began to totter towards Tucka. 'Mommy!' he said.

'Get away from me, you monster!' she squealed and aimed a sharp kick at him. The kick sent him rolling across the floor in a ball that got smaller and smaller as it rolled. And finally it disappeared altogether.

There was a moment of stunned silence.

'Tucka! Please stop the machine before we're killed!' Hermux pleaded.

But Tucka was already occupied with trying to piece together the burned fragments of the formula. 'Can't you see that I'm busy!' she hissed.

'I'll take those, Tucka!' someone commanded.

Tucka looked up.

Blanda Nergup stood in the doorway, breathing hard. Her hair was an even bigger mess than usual. 'I'll take those!' she repeated. 'They're mine.'

She had picked up Tucka's gun and held it firmly in one hand.

'Don't be ridiculous, Nergup!' sputtered Tucka. 'Who invited you out here anyway? Put that gun down at once!'

251

The two women glared at each other.

The clock ticked loudly. The bar of the mousetrap had reached the top of its arc. It was ready to snap. Hermux threw himself towards the toolbox with a burst of energy that could only have come from the moon plant. He yanked the lid open and felt frantically inside for his snips. They were right on top. He grasped them firmly and cut the wire that ran from the harness to the clock. It gave with a taut snap. The wire sprang back and cut Hermux sharply across his cheek.

'Ow!' he cried and felt the warm blood wetting his fur.

The clock stopped.

'Put the gun down immediately, Nergup! Or you're fired!' blustered Tucka.

'Fired? No, Tucka, I'm not fired. I quit!'

Nergup removed her thick glasses and tossed them on the floor.

'She really does look better without those glasses,' thought Hermux, rubbing his cheek. 'If she could just do something about her posture ...'

No sooner had he thought it, than Blanda Nergup stood up. She rose taller and taller until she towered over Tucka. She brought her free hand to her hair and loosened the pins that held it in its peculiar shape. Then she pulled, and the hair came off in her hand, revealing a head of short, sleek golden fur.

'Ortolina Perriflot!' scowled Tucka. 'You'll regret this!'

'Now hand me the formula,' said Ortolina firmly. 'It rightfully belongs to the Perriflot Institute!'

Tucka gathered the fragments together and dutifully carried them to Ortolina.

'You're right,' she said apologetically. 'It does belong to

252

you. So take a good look at it!' And with that she tossed the handful in Ortolina's face, grabbing for the gun and throwing all of her weight against her willowy opponent. Ortolina staggered back, coughing and sneezing. The two of them crashed noisily into the control panel of the U-Babe 2000, which came to life with a loud clang. Lights flashed. Buzzers buzzed. And a treatment capsule slid into view and opened.

Tucka and Ortolina struggled ferociously back and forth for the gun. Finally Tucka gave a triumphant cry and broke away from Ortolina. She staggered back on the platform, clutching the gun in her hand.

'Now we'll see whose formula this is!' she threatened icily. But even as she spoke, Tucka's stiletto heel caught the edge of the platform, and she was pitched backwards into the U-Babe 2000's waiting capsule.

She struggled to sit up and aimed the gun directly at Ortolina. 'Goodbye, Perriflot!' she said. 'Money can't buy everything!'

That's when Hermux threw the snips. They sailed through the air and scored a direct hit on the control panel's large red button.

Instantly the top of the capsule dropped shut, knocking Tucka flat inside. Then with an explosive burst of air, the capsule and Tucka vanished inside the U-Babe 2000.

Moments later Hermux could see Tucka's catsuit being vacuumed through the clothing tubes. And he could see the body icons flashing on the control panel. The full-body sculpt was still set for a muscular, male hamster. A scream of outrage echoed through the lab. And Hermux thought he could hear the whine of a sewing-machine at work.

Chapter 74

VISITING HOURS

In Hermux's dream he was trapped in a capsule in the U-Babe 2000. He was being sucked through a dizzying, endless maze of tubes. Finally the capsule opened. A metal rotisserie arm reached inside for him and pinned him down while another arm began to tickle his face with Blanda Nergup's wig.

Hermux woke himself up with a mighty sneeze.

It was broad daylight. He was in his own bed. In his own apartment. And something was tickling his face.

It was Terfle. She peered at him from the pillow.

Hermux sat up happily.

'Terfle!' he cried. 'Where have you been? I was so worried about you!'

He picked her up carefully and without bothering to put on his robe or his slippers, he ran to his study.

It was still a terrible wreck. But in the bright sunshine and with Terfle perched on his paw, it looked just grand. Terfle looked tired. One of her bright red wings was chipped. Her antennae seemed a little out of alignment. And when Hermux looked very closely he saw what looked like tiny bits of confetti stuck to her feet.

'Oh, Terfle!' he chided. 'What on earth have you been doing?'

Terfle stroked Hermux's paw with one of her tiny feet. But she said nothing.

Very gently he put her inside her cage. 'I'll get you some fresh food and water,' he told her and rushed to the kitchen with her bowls. But by the time he got back, Terfle had climbed up on to her perch and was sound asleep. In fact it seemed to Hermux that she was even snoring.

'Well, you can tell me everything when you wake up,' he said. He stood for a moment and gazed fondly at his little sleeping friend. Then he closed the door to her cage, quietly pulled the shades, and tiptoed from the room.

'Oh, my goodness,' he exclaimed, looking at his watch. 'It's very late. Visiting hours at the hospital are nearly over. I've got to see Ms Perflinger and make sure she's all right. I have so much to tell her. And ask.'

He dressed hastily and rushed out. He stopped at the shop and retrieved Ms Perflinger's watch from the 'Will Call' shelf. He bought a bouquet of roses and forget-me-nots on the street and then boarded the trolley for the hospital.

As he rode along he opened the box and gazed thoughtfully at Ms Perflinger's watch. He was relieved to see that it still kept perfect time. It seemed so long ago that she had stood before him in the shop with the battered watch.

At the hospital he walked proudly up the broad stairs and asked for her room number. The stitches in his cheek still ached. And he walked with a slight limp from twisting his ankle, but he felt so proud as he stepped off the elevator.

He had managed to save Ms Perflinger.

Or at least he had helped to save her.

He rehearsed what he planned to say to her. How intensely he had worried about her. The fondness that he felt for her. The hope he had that they might be more than friends.

It was with a fast-beating heart that he opened the door and stepped into her room.

He was disappointed to see that she was not alone. A lanky mouse with a cane sat smoking a pipe. A thick white cast covered one of his legs.

'Oh, Mr Tantamoq!' Ms Perflinger said brightly. 'How very nice of you to come. Turfip, this is Mr Tantamoq. The watchmaker who saved my life. Mr Tantamoq, this is Dr Dandiffer—my fiancé.'

'Congratulations!' he managed to say through the sudden blackness that enveloped him. 'To both of you! What a surprise!'

'It's hard to believe, isn't it?' Linka asked. 'From the jaws of death to wedding plans in a single day! My head is still reeling.'

'Mine too,' admitted Hermux. 'Do you mind if I sit down for a moment?'

As he sank into a chair he felt a crushing weight settle on his shoulders. He knew he had to get out of her room before he burst into hopeless tears.

'I've brought these flowers for you. And your watch,' he said, placing the box carefully on the edge of her bed.

She opened it immediately.

'It looks perfect!' she exclaimed. She slipped her watch on to her slim wrist and admired it. 'You've done a wonderful job with it.'

'It keeps excellent time,' said Hermux wistfully. 'And I see that it's time for me to go. I wish you a speedy recovery, Ms Perflinger. And I hope you'll be very happy. I wish you both all the best.'

Hermux staggered out into the hall and pulled the door closed quickly behind him. He realized that he still clutched the bouquet tightly in his paw.

As he passed the nurse's station, he placed the flowers on the counter.

'These are from Ms Perflinger,' he told the nurse on duty. 'She thanks you for all the special care.'

'Why, how thoughtful!' said the nurse. 'She's certainly a fine young mouse. It's hard to imagine what she's been through. Say! You're Mr Tantamoq, aren't you? I saw your photo in the paper this morning. You're quite the hero!'

A red light flashed angrily on the counter and a buzzer sounded repeatedly.

The nurse pursed her lips in irritation.

'Never mind that!' she said. 'It's that Mertslin woman. And she can just wait!'

Chapter 75
ALL IS REVEALED

'And so Tucka won't go to jail after all,' said Mirrin, sipping her tea.

'No,' said Hermux. 'What she did with Mennus wasn't illegal. She claims she had a legitimate research contract with him. She had no idea he was stealing the formula. And I'm making an effort to believe her.'

'But what about leaving you to die in the mousetrap?'

'Well, the detective in charge of the case tells me we can't really prosecute her for rudeness.'

'Rudeness? That was way beyond rudeness.'

'Well, it's her word against mine. She claims that she didn't realize we were in any real danger. Anyway it's over. We're alive. And I'm willing to let bygones be bygones. Besides she must have suffered a lot, losing her tail in the U-Babe and getting sewn up into a hamster's body. Of course, Tucka will come out on top. Apparently she's hired a writer, and she's staying busy in the hospital dictating her memoirs while the doctors remove all the stitches.'

'I'm still a little shocked that it was Pup Schoonagliffen all along,' said Mirren. 'He seemed like such a nice, thoughtful young mole.'

'Even knowing what I know now, I still miss Pup,' said Hermux sadly. 'I really liked him. He knew so much about so many things. I thought he was my friend. And I wasn't the only one. People told Pup everything. He was always willing to listen. And he was always ready to help. I wonder if any of what seemed good about Pup was real. Or if he was just a creation of Mennus. Between the two of them they knew everything. Spies at the Perriflot Institute, at Tucka's, and on Dandiffer's expedition. Mennus or Pup or whoever he was could watch everyone. Tucka, Ortolina, me, Jervutz. And if he couldn't watch us, we were more than willing to tell him anything he needed to know. We were just small pieces in his game. He knew Dandiffer would be back. He planned to use Linka to lure him out to the Last Resort. Dandiffer was the last loose thread. As soon as he was snipped, Mennus would only have Tucka to deal with. As mad as she is at me and Ortolina, she knows we saved her life.'

'And Ortolina was involved in this all along?'

'She realized that there was a spy at the Perriflot Institute. And she knew it was no coincidence that Tucka was cooking up the Millennium Project. She wanted to be where she could keep an eye on her. So she disguised herself as Blanda Nergup and talked herself into a job with Tucka. Fortunately for me and Linka.'

'And what will you do now? Do you think you'll ever get over losing Linka?'

'Ah, Linka,' sighed Hermux. 'No, I don't suppose I ever will. Whenever I see a plane in the sky, I'll think of her. And

I'll wonder where she is just then and what might have been. But I've learned such a lot. About love. About beauty. About friendship. I don't regret any of it. And that reminds me. I brought you a little souvenir of my adventure.'

'What, Hermux?' Mirrin asked. 'A free sample of Tucka's shampoo?'

'No. Something a little more special I think. I'm not making any promises,' he continued. 'It's just a hunch I have. When the police arrived at the Last Resort, there was a lot of chaos and confusion and waiting around while they rounded up Mennus's crew. No one was paying much attention to me. So when I spotted a broken piece of the flask that Mennus dropped, I just bent down to tie my shoe and slipped it into my pocket. And here it is.'

Hermux removed a jewellery box from his jacket pocket.

'Now I need to get a glass of water,' he said, getting up and going into the kitchen. 'You know, if Mennus had gotten his hands on Dandiffer's journal, things might have ended very differently. The youth formula is much too powerful to drink. He would have known that if he had read the journal. I wish I could say that keeping the journal a secret was part of some ingenious strategy of mine. But the truth is that I just forgot to tell Pup where I'd hidden it. And he was so keen to get the formula that he forgot to ask.'

Hermux returned with a small glass of water which he placed in front of him on the coffee table. He opened the jewellery box. A curved shard of glass lay on the midnight blue velvet lining. A rusty stain was all that remained of the formula. Hermux lifted the broken glass carefully and dropped it gently into the water. The stain released a tiny blood-red

260

cloud that blossomed momentarily and then dissipated.

'Now,' said Hermux to Mirrin. 'I want you to lie back and keep your eyes closed.' He removed a spotless white handkerchief from his pocket, unfolded it and dipped it into the water. He refolded it into a compress and placed it over Mirrin's eyes.

'Keep your eyes closed and hold very still.'

He sat down next to Mirrin and took out his pocket watch.

'What is it, Hermux?' she asked. 'What is happening?'

'I'm not sure exactly,' he said. 'Let's wait one more minute. You know, Mirrin, you've been very patient with me over the years. You've opened my eyes to a lot of new things. Like your paintings and the opera and this idea of trying to be a careful observer of the world. The last few weeks in particular I've given a lot of thought to the idea of *beauty*. I've never really taken the time to do that before. And I've come to agree with you. I do have a sense of beauty. And I have finally thought of something that I would find very beautiful. Something that I would like to see.'

'What is it? Tell me!'

'It's this,' said Hermux, checking his watch.

He peeled away his handkerchief from Mirrin's eyes. And he helped her to her feet.

'Now,' he said hopefully. 'Open your eyes.'

And Mirrin did.

She stood motionless for a moment, and then she walked very slowly towards the window without saying a word. She looked out at her garden which she had not seen for three years. She saw the honeysuckle on the gate. She saw the grass that needed cutting. She saw the peonies fallen over from the

261

afternoon rain. And when she turned away from the window she saw her dear friend Hermux standing beside her.

'I can see,' she said simply.

'And that is every bit as beautiful as I imagined,' said Hermux with a smile.

ABOUT THE AUTHOR

Michael Hoeye lives with his wife Martha and their elderly
cat Lionel in a stone cottage in Oregon. They enjoy the
company of 9 big oak trees, 6 bigger fir trees,
3 fat squirrels, a noisy family of woodpeckers, and a
travelling circus of nuthatches, stellar jays, crows, finches,
and robins. *Time Stops for No Mouse* is his first book.

Portrait by Virginia Flynn

Acknowledgements

Many people helped bring this book to life. Thanks first of all to the brave bookstores that believed in it. Thanks to Gloria Borg Olds at Broadway Books in Portland; to Tonyia Vining, and David and Beth Henkes at University Bookstore in Bellevue, Washington; and to Bobbie Tichenor at Annie Bloom's Books in Portland. Thanks to the wonderful people at Publishers Group West, especially Harry Kirchener, Heather Cameron and John Mesjak. Thanks also for the encouragement of early readers Dorothy and Bill Kucha, the Parker-Lavine family and Rhonda Coleman. Thanks for invaluable creative work and inspiration to Dale Champlin, Ann Marra, Tim Ely, Virginia Flynn, Richie Williamson, David Vogel, Lily Hazlewood, Patricia Tate and Martha Moore. Thanks to Barbara Roether, Marc H. Glick, and to my agents Marilyn Marlow, Elizabeth Harding, Dave Barbor and Brandon Vanover of Curtis Brown, Ltd. And very special thanks to Nancy Paulsen, Douglas Whiteman and everyone at Penguin Putnam Books for Young Readers.

A very special thank you to
my dear old friend Lionel for many years of devoted
companionship and for his keen insight into the workings of
the animal mind.

And to Dinah (R.I.P.) for tutoring me privately in the
complexities of the prima donna's world view.